PROJECT
SCARECROW

Natalie Buske Thomas

ISBN-13: 978-0615869513

ISBN-10: 0615869513

This book is a work of fiction.
All events and dialog are for
entertainment purposes only and do not
necessarily represent the author's views

To Brent, Cassandra, Nicholas and
Savannah

RESEARCH CREDITS

Sunday Afternoon on the Porch: Reflections of a Small Town in Iowa, 1939-1942 Photographs by Everett W. Kuntz, Text by Jim Heynen, University of Iowa Press, Iowa City ISBN 978-1-58729-653-6

Abandoned: Now Stutter My Orphan by Jerry Halvorson, ISBN 0-9664894-1-1

The Marshall Cavendish Illustrated Encyclopedia of World War 1, Brigadier Peter Young Editor in Chief, ISBN 0-86307-191-0

AEF Casualty Handling Procedures www.WorldWar1.com© 1998-2000, The Great War Society

Another Part of the Twenties by Paul A. Carter, Columbia University Press, ISBN 0-231-04134-9

Answering the Call: The U.S. Army Nurse Corps, 1917-1919: A Commemorative Tribute to Military Nursing in World War I Lisa M. Budreau, Office of the Surgeon General, Office of Medical History (U.S. Army), Richard M. Prior, Government Printing Office, Agency Publisher: Defense Dept., Army, Office of the Surgeon General, Office of Medical History GPO Stock Number: 008-023-00136-7 ISBN: 9780160817243

Pershing by Jim Lacey, The Great Generals Series, Palgrave Macmillan ISBN 0-230-60383-1

AUTHOR'S WORKS

The Serena Wilcox Mysteries

The Serena Wilcox Time Travel Trilogy
Project Scarecrow Vol. 7, Trilogy #3, Book #1

The Serena Wilcox Dystopian Trilogy
Bluebird Flown Vol. 6, Trilogy #2, Book #3
Covert Coffee Vol. 5, Trilogy #2, Book #2
Angels Mark Vol. 4, Trilogy #2, Book #1

The Serena Wilcox Mysteries: Books 1, 2 & 3
Camp Conviction Vol. 3, Trilogy #1, Book #3
Virtual Memories, Vol. 2, Trilogy #1, Book #2
Gene Play Vol. 1, Trilogy #1, Book #1

Other Works

Oil paintings (most notably *Savannah Reading
in the Butterfly Garden*), Books outside of The Serena
Wilcox Mysteries: *Fred Born Gifted, The Miracle
Dulcimer, The Magic Camera* Natalie is also a
singer/songwriter, public speaker and entertainer.

www.NatalieBuskeThomas.com

1

"I'm Serena Wilcox, former private detective, wife, and mother of three. I did investigative work for President Ann Kinji, as you already know."

"Yes, we know who you are." Agent Estep folded his arms over his chest and extended his legs far out in front of his chair, crossed at the ankles.

"Agent Estep and I go way back. Don't let his attitude fool you, we're buddies." Serena winked at him. "We worked together during Operation Covert Coffee."

Estep addressed the group without budging from his slouched nearly-prone sprawl. "Who here doesn't already know Serena Wilcox?"

A small wiry man raised his hand.

Estep scoffed. "One guy. You're giving us this spiel for one guy?"

Serena ignored him and resumed reading from her notes. "Now that President Ann's term has ended, she is ready to launch the Gödel Solution Institute where she is owner and CEO. You are of course already aware of this, as you are the first members of the GSI board of directors. President Ann—I think I speak for all of us when I say that she'll always be President to us—asked me to kick things off because she wanted you to see the person who is doing the traveling. I suppose she thought you'd keep me safe if you saw my face." Serena paused for laughter but none was forthcoming. She continued, "Thank you for this opportunity to pioneer in time travel crime investigation. I can't even begin to express what this means to me."

Serena sat down amid a smattering of polite applause. The lone person who hadn't previously met Serena popped up and took her place at the front of the board room.

He took a few sips of water even though he hadn't yet said a word. Then he studied his audience, which was composed of about fifty-fifty Covert Coffee leftovers (Ann Kinji's investigative team) and his own people (mathematicians, technicians and scientists): the dark-and-unruly-haired quick-tempered Agent Estep, the 40-something high-energy petite brunette Serena, the infamously burned agent-turned-national-hero Beav, the red-headed curly-haired lass from Ireland, Jo, former agent (and briefly Vice President) Lehman, Ann's contact Professor Dr. Kendra Wellington and five members of Eduardo's hand-picked team, Roger McCloy, Gentry Davis, Malirah Cravitz, Jorgi Gorantisch and James Edison Spector. He nodded to his team, they returned the greeting, and then he finally spoke. "I'm here to brief you on Project Scarecrow. I'm Eduardo Martin."

Eduardo paused to smile at them. Everyone smiled back. He continued. "I assume that you are familiar with the Manhattan Project. In 1939, farther back than we can currently time travel, Albert Einstein sent a letter, drafted by prominent physicists of the time, to President Franklin Delano Roosevelt. Einstein warned of a weapon being built by Nazi Germany that was more powerful than the world had ever known. He was referring to the atomic bomb. The course of history was changed: the United States developed an atomic research program using the code name The Manhattan Project, all because of Einstein's letter. What if I told you that another such letter existed? A letter that also has the power to change the course of history?"

"Einstein wrote another letter?" Serena asked.

"I didn't say that." Eduardo drank the rest of his water as if his brief speech had drained him dry.

Jorgi Gorantisch's voice boomed from the back of the room. He was a man who never needed a microphone, and given his six-foot-five two-hundred-thirty pound presence, he was seen as easily as he was heard. The fact that Jorgi was typically a girls' name was an irony that no one ever brought to his attention. "Forget Einstein."

Beav, whose foot had fallen asleep and whose stomach had been rumbling for the past several minutes, entered the conversation. "Then what is this about?"

Eduardo picked at his thin mustache before speaking. "The only connection between what I'm saying now and Albert Einstein is that I want you to focus on the letter; how one letter was the catalyst to monumental change. There's been another pivotal point in history involving a letter, but unlike Einstein's, it will never lead to world change because it was never delivered to the right people."

Serena raised her hand and then spoke without waiting for an invitation. "To be clear, this letter has nothing to do with atomic bombs, the Manhattan Project, or Albert Einstein." As soon as Serena said this she heard Estep groan. She mouthed, "What?"

Eduardo's mustache picking escalated to the point that his upper lip was now stretched tight across his already taut face. "To be clear, no it does not."

Beav was a man who kept his own time and was not typically hurried by any outside stimulus, but at this moment his stomach was complaining of hunger. He prompted, "Our first project is to send Serena back to the year that the letter was written and see that it's delivered to the right people?"

Eduardo's face reddened. He stopped picking at his mustache and reached for his now-empty water glass. He scowled at the glass before directing an even deeper scowl at Beav. "My usage of the word 'letter' is metaphorical."

Beav fought back the urge to rub the skin of his own upper lip as he watched

Eduardo's mustache pulling act. Beav was sporting a goatee these days. He also had long tresses that he had pulled back with elastic and had topped off with a bandana that brought out the gypsy in him. If Ann or Serena were to request that he wear a monkey suit, so be it. Meanwhile he sported a sleeveless t-shirt and his favorite denim.

Beav's appearance belied his formal manner of discourse. His rebuttal to Eduardo was unhurried, his empty stomach temporarily forgotten. "While I understand what you are saying about using the word 'letter' metaphorically, I am at a loss about what you do mean in a literal sense. I too am frequently led astray by my own musings. However, if we can pin down…"

Agent Estep snarled, "Can we please get back on track? Some of us have to get back to our day jobs."

Estep never missed an opportunity to rub salt in Beav's wounds. Regardless of Beav's hero-celebrity status, he had no hope of ever being reinstated. On the contrary, Estep was still in the agency's good graces and even basked in the loyalty of the top brass. To top it off, Agent Estep was awarded a ridiculous number of sparkly medals following Operation Covert Coffee. Estep had, after all, carried President Ann Kinji out of harm's way—literally in his arms, like a prince saving the princess, a story that the media would never tire of packaging into yet another feature. Beav couldn't avoid seeing Estep's digital smug mug for weeks on end, and now he was up close and personal with him again on a regular basis.

Eduardo had fetched himself a new glass of water while Estep and Beav stewed, refusing to look at each other. If Eduardo had picked up on the tension he

9

didn't show it. He launched into the rest of his speech uninterrupted.

"We are limited in our time travel by what we call the memory window. You see, each of us is born with a brain capable of nearly limitless possibilities to store sensory input, experiences, data and memories. Most of us have a relatively short memory window of about five years, give or take, meaning that we don't remember much that happened beyond five years into the past and we have no access to the 'memory', or shall we say 'awareness', of future events.

Whereas, in individuals thought to have psychic ability, the areas of the brain that are completely untapped for most of us are accessible to those who 'see' the future. We now believe that there's a simple scientific explanation to explain psychic phenomenon: Brain damage, birth defects, and anomalies can cause a spillage, an access point, into the areas of the brain that store future events.

We have discovered that human brains contain our entire life maps, from the womb to the grave. Normally we can't see much beyond the five year memory window I mentioned. People with remarkable minds, most often due to brain anomalies and abnormalities, may have a photographic memory or might see glimpses of the future.

But what if we could access the entire memory window? What I mean by this is; what if we could tap into the entire life span of a person? For example, if we had access to a person who is over one hundred years old we could acquire quite a record, at least from that person's perspective, of up to one hundred years into the past.

Keep in mind that we'd only have data that this individual has heard, read, viewed, sensed, and so on. Not all impressions are subjective; some are spot-on accurate because they come from official sources or verifiable events, but we do have to proceed with caution. For example, the memory of having read a letter would give us a reliable databank of what someone actually communicated, whereas the memory of a verbal conversation could be faulty due to the listener not hearing the spoken word correctly, or misinterpreting the meaning of what was said.

And what works for the past can also work for the future. If we go in the other direction, we can tap into a newborn's brain and see into the future as far as that particular newborn's lifespan. Assuming that the newborn in question leads a normal healthy life and dies from natural causes, a single subject will offer us a memory window of about one hundred years into the future. These days it's not uncommon to discover lifespans of one hundred and fifteen years or more.

I notice that some of you look dismayed. Don't worry; no one is harmed by brain tapping. We need only a laser incision to insert the sensor. The sensor converts brain impressions into usable data. The data is then processed by my esteemed colleagues here." Eduardo gestured toward his team.

When no one responded he resumed. "The science has been with us all along but we had no way of conversion. With the emergence of the digital age it was a short hop, skip and a jump from our understanding of the laws of physics to our ability to mine for the information we needed to make time travel possible.

We have already collected data from thousands of subjects, and thirty-three time travel pioneers have already gone before you, Serena Wilcox. We have done it, we have mastered it. My fellow physicist Jorgi was misguiding you when he told you to forget Einstein. No, my friends, we can't do that. It all goes back to Einstein."

Eduardo stopped himself and looked at Serena, who was staring up at him with her lips slightly parted as if she were about to speak. He hastily said, "Before you ask, no, this is not about the letter. I'm talking about Einstein's field equations published in 1915; a little something called general relativity."

Eduardo noted the blank expressions on every face in the room, excepting those from his own team. "Hold on." He moved to the presentation tablet.

The tablet's stylus had been misplaced so he used his fingertip to write an equation: (curvature of space-time) = (mass-energy density) $* 8 \, pi \, G \, / \, c^4$. He spun around to face the group with the wide-open rapidly-blinking gaze of someone who believes that his point has been made. However, his gaze was met by droopy-lidded eyes that blinked slowly, like those of a reptile in an observation tank.

Eduardo sighed. "I don't know how I can make this any clearer. If you aren't familiar with basic physics there's not much I can do to help you understand the science of time travel."

Malirah Cravitz stood up. "May I try?" She carried herself to the presentation tablet on her long dancer's legs. Her dark skin in contrast to her canary yellow suit dress, the afro that floated in a six-inch halo around her head, and the shimmery crimson lipstick cast her as a runway fashion model instead of the physicist that she most certainly was.

It had been a battle to get the male-dominated world of science to take Malirah seriously, but she had done it without giving up any of her glamour. Her intimidating height helped. Only three men in the board room were taller than she, and Eduardo was especially dwarfed by her. He stepped aside without another word.

Malirah drew a picture of a funnel. "Let's start with a cone shape, like an e-collar that prevents a dog from licking his wounds."

She drew a hound with sad eyes, wearing a lampshade around his neck. Then she shook her head so hard that her afro kept moving long after her head stopped shaking. She scrubbed out the picture of the dog. "I have a better analogy. Think of a hovercraft park. Riders can make an almost infinite number of different paths, while always going back to where they started from. Gravity brings all skaters back to the same common point eventually.

Even though each rider follows an entirely different path, they are all riding on the same curve; let's call it the same timeline. Imagine that time and space are like a hovercraft park, and we are all riders. Some of us are in the past (either because we have traveled there, or because we live there), some of us are in the present—the fixed point where riders start and stop—and some of us are in the future (again, either because we have traveled there or because we live there). But none of us have left the curve, 'us' meaning every human being who has ever lived, and *will* ever live.

Now, of course, the humans who have already died will never have the opportunity to be in our present or our future unless we go back in time and use time travel technology to bring them into the present or into the future. Conversely, people who have not yet been born can't show up in our present or in the past unless we—or they—use time travel.

Imagine that riders in the past have limited paths that they can travel, and can never reach the fixed point that we call the present. Imagine that the same is true for riders of the future. But for all of us living in the present, we can access the fixed point and part of each side of the curve—on the path destined for us. However, we only get one ride. Now imagine that we are all time travelers. Not only can we access the entire curve, but we can take more than one turn—we get an infinite number of rides, theoretically."

Serena gasped. "Are you saying that we've found a way to become immortal?"

Malirah's afro bobbed as she vigorously shook her head. She held up a manicured hand for emphasis. "No, I didn't say that."

Eduardo attempted to regain control of the podium. He addressed the room as a whole and avoided making direct eye contact with Serena. "If you have an interest in physics, by all means do your own research or talk to one of us. We love to talk shop and we'll gladly bend your ear."

Beav raised his hand and waited for permission to speak. Malirah cocked her fingers in loaded-gun fashion and fired. Beav said, "If this is going to go on much longer I suggest that we take a lunch break."

Malirah's afro bobbed. "No, I'm done with my bit. I'll turn it back over to Eduardo." She strode back to her seat and managed to sit gracefully even though the chair was too small for her.

Eduardo assured them. "I'm on the wrap-up. Let's hold off on lunch until I'm finished. Back on topic, I wanted to mention that The Gödel metric is an exact solution of the Einstein field equations. I thought you might find it interesting to know where the Gödel Solution Institute got its name. And that's where we'll leave the science of time travel." He paused mysteriously. "I'd be remiss if I didn't mention the grandfather paradox."

Eduardo's hand shot straight to his mustache for a twist, tug and pull when he saw that Serena had opened her mouth to speak.

"I think I know this one," said Serena. "If I go back in time and kill my grandfather before he meets my grandmother, I'll never be born, meaning that I couldn't grow up and time travel, so Grandpa is safe. It's a paradox, like what came first, the chicken or the egg."

"No, it's not like the chicken and the…" Eduardo's mustache tango went up-tempo for a few mesmerizing seconds before he let Serena's ignorance slide. "But you understand the concept of the grandfather paradox well enough. Here at the institute we believe that the past cannot be changed to the point in which it will throw the curve out of orbit. I like Malirah's visual of a hovercraft park. We believe that we can join the riders, we can interact with them, and we can mix things up a great deal, but we can't remove any riders from the curve. This isn't a code of ethics, but a law of science. It is impossible to create a paradox: the universe does not allow it."

"God doesn't allow it." Serena smiled.

Eduardo gave his mustache such a yank that the hair follicles were likely to be permanently damaged. "Yes, well… Let's stay on track, shall we? I need for you to hear what I'm saying. While we don't believe that we are in any credible danger of a paradox, we do believe that we can alter the course of history, and that the changes that we make may have unintended and undesirable effects.

21

Remember the hovercraft riders? As long as the riders are contained within the curve, we can add new riders if we wish, therefore the current riders may be then be thrown off their original intended paths. The universe, science, or whatever you choose to believe, allows this. Do you understand what I'm trying to tell you, Serena?"

Serena nodded. "You are telling me to stay in my own lane."

Eduardo worried his sore upper lip until specks of blood appeared. "Ms. Wilcox, I have my doubts as to whether or not you can manage time travel without adversely changing the course of history."

Agent Estep snickered and coughed.

Serena protested, "But isn't the whole point of me traveling so that I can change history? Or is my investigation an intelligence gathering mission only?"

Eduardo glanced upward and held his gaze for several long seconds. Then he locked eyes with Serena Wilcox. "You'll have your assignment. Stick to the plan and avoid your grandfather."

Serena whined, "I thought you said that the grandfather paradox is impossible. Now you're saying I have to worry about creating a paradox? What level of 'bad' would this be: 'the whole planet could implode' bad or 'global warming just got warmer' bad? What would a paradox do exactly?"

Eduardo drank the rest of his second glass of water in one long draught. He said, "This is an excellent time to conclude our first board meeting. Enjoy your lunch."

Everyone sprang from their chairs except for Serena. She remained seated and called out, "But you didn't answer my question."

Eduardo was swallowed by the group of hungry board members as they exited all at once. When he emerged at her side he bent down to rasp in her ear, "Ask God."

2

The Gödel Solution Institute was located on a forty-five acre parcel of land that was previously part of the old Department of Natural Resources restoration program: the DNR had paid farmers not to use their land; the property was then seeded with varieties of wild grasses and flowering plants indigenous to the area. The property was not available.

Ann Kinji's reign as a beloved American President afforded her anything she asked for now that she was a private citizen. In this instance she didn't even have to ask. A committee of representatives from the DNR offered the parcel to her as soon as her intention to buy land was made public. The original landowner was more than happy to sell the property to the DNR, and Congress unanimously approved gifting the deed to the Gödel Solution Institute. Billed as an organization designed to protect the interests of all humankind, it was not in anyone's political interest to disapprove Ann's petition to secure the land for GSI. While some may have harbored resentment or reluctance, those feelings never surfaced. From the outside looking in, it appeared as if absolutely everyone in the United States, and abroad as well, was in favor of building The Gödel Solution Institute.

Due to the unanimous support and the butt-kissing that had reached Olympian levels worthy of extreme-sport gold, Ann had expected that the ground-breaking for GSI would be swift and uneventful. Unfortunately Mother Nature had interfered. There was one weather-related delay after another until the timeline for the opening had become a nail-biter. At the last minute the project came together, complete with a tastefully painted interior, a fully stocked lounge, and high-end décor adorning every nook and cranny. And none of this cost the public a dime. Everything was donated by prominent artisans, designers and builders—it was the Who's Who of elite society as they competed to get their names on the plaques that papered the institute's lobby walls.

To celebrate the ground-breaking all sponsors were to also attend a lavish self-serving banquet with Ann Kinji as their guest of honor. It was understood that Ann would be attending, as Ann had graciously accepted public appearances as one of her roles as President and CEO of the institute. She and her husband Ted had even taken ballroom dance lessons to surprise and delight at these affairs (this was not much of a surprise after all; the media had already broken the story about the dance lessons and had even taped several sessions).

Ann wasn't bent out of shape about the public relations aspect of her new job—with the right attitude these events were a perk. She even looked forward to her new social life. The ground-breaking gala was to be only the first event of many more to come.

However, something happened at her fist gala that was troubling Ann. She couldn't put her finger on what was off about the incident but she knew that she should trust her intuition and look into what was going on. While she and Ted were mixing it up on the dance floor, party guests were whooping and applauding, surrounding the dance floor on all sides. Cameras flashed constantly, creating a strobe light effect. Yet there was one noticeable clutch of people who weren't cheering them on.

From Ann's perspective on the raised dance platform she had the vantage point of seeing the entire room. The lone dissenters apparently didn't realize that, while they were well-hidden by the throng of party-goers from the ground level, from Ann's position on the dance platform she could see them as clearly as if they were standing two feet away from her.

Unbeknownst to them, Ann utilized the slow movements of a long waltz to observe the suspicious group.

Shortly after the event Ann had called upon Serena and Beav to look into it. Ann anticipated that it would be relatively easy for the pair of them to solve the trivial mystery of the suspicious party guests at the ground-breaking gala but she still hadn't heard from either of them. Knowing that both were on the GSI campus this morning she seized the opportunity to request their presence.

Beav arrived first with a pouch of tuna in one hand and two leafy stalks of kale in the other hand. Ann invited him to finish his lunch while they waited for Serena to arrive. They waited for fifteen minutes before Ann buzzed her secretary.

Ruby, a golden-haired seventy-four year old woman who could run circles around staff members five decades her junior, arrived at her door. "I haven't been able to reach her. I've left her three voice mails." Ruby disappeared down the hall and was almost back at her post in the lobby when she called, "Never mind, she's here now. I'll send her in."

Serena turned up almost before Ruby finished her sentence. Ann embraced her in a brief squeeze-and-release power hug and then greeted her with an admonishment. "Long time, my friend. I missed you at the ground-breaking, and the gala, and apparently you never turn your phone on."

Serena's sheepish look gave her away.

Ann raised an eyebrow. "You still don't have a phone do you?"

Serena shook her head. "No. I got the message through Estep."

"How often does this happen? I can only imagine how much Estep enjoys taking messages for you," Ann chuckled.

31

"I'll get a phone, it's on my list. I hope I haven't kept you waiting long."

"Not a problem. The delay gave Beav time to eat his lunch. I assume you already ate?"

"Yes, I'm good. I'm guessing that this isn't a social visit. You want to know if we made any progress digging into the gala situation."

"Yes, I was wondering about that. Typically you keep me informed. I must say that I'm rather surprised that I had to track you down."

"I've been busy preparing for my new gig. I didn't realize how much training they'd have me do. But besides that, I didn't contact you because there's nothing to report. They weren't on the guest list. Beav couldn't find anything either."

"Nothing at all?" Ann sat behind her desk and motioned for Serena to sit in one of the guest chairs.

Beav, who had been sitting far longer than he was accustomed to, between the board meeting and now this near siesta in Ann's office, struggled to shake off his groggy after-lunch fog. "I wouldn't say 'nothing at all'. I did find out who they are."

Ann waited a few seconds before prompting him. "Well, who are they?"

Beav groaned. "You aren't going to like this. I used the facility's surveillance cameras and the footage that your security team had from their standard sweeps. From there it was easy to get an ID. They're in the system, all nine of them."

"Are they agents, politicians, or what?" Ann scowled. Why hadn't she recognized any of them? "What system?"

Serena answered. "The prison system."

"Why were felons at the gala and what were they chewing the fat about?" Ann grabbed the nearest pencil from her mug of writing utensils and chewed on the eraser. It was her first eraser gnawing since the days of Operation Covert Coffee. She flinched when she realized what she was doing and flung the eraser--pencil and all--into the trash bin.

Serena shrugged. "Sorry, we have no idea why they were there or what they were doing. Beav's been working on it. I've been too preoccupied by the travel training."

Ann relaxed her posture, visibly switching gears. "How is that going?"

"Fine I guess. So far they are teaching me physics, or trying to. I never made it that far in science so it's a lost cause. I haven't even seen the time machine yet."

Ann exchanged an alarmed look with Beav. "Time machine?"

"They haven't shown it to me. I'm anxious to see what I'm in for. I hope it's easy for me to drive, or operate, or whatever it is I have to do to get it to go. I'd like to at least see what it looks like. Does it steer like a ship? Do I have to memorize a panel of buttons or something?" Serena was so lost in her own thoughts that she didn't notice the frantic gesturing between Ann and Beav.

Beav spoke in a tone of voice that people use when they are talking over the heads of a child. "I think the time machine part of the training is on the schedule for, um, the end of the w…" Ann shook her head vigorously. "…month."

Serena gasped. "The end of the month? Why so long? I thought my first mission was coming up in a couple of weeks."

Ann stood up and clapped Serena gently on the shoulder. "I'm sure it will all work out. I've taken up enough of your time. Please take the rest of the day off for yourself and your family."

35

Serena grinned. "Oh thank you! As much as I'd love to stay and chat, it sure has been a long week. I'd love to go home. Beav, do you need a ride?"

Beav waved his hand dismissively. "I'm good."

Serena held the door open for him. "Aren't you leaving?"

Beav glanced at Ann who quickly looked away. "Um, no, I think I'll stay on for a bit. I'll brainstorm about why those prisoners were at the gala."

Serena looked from Beav to Ann and back again. She knew something was up but her desire to go home overrode any curiosity she had about what they were doing.

As soon as Serena was out of earshot Ann said, "Shut the door."

Beav locked the door for good measure and pulled his chair close to Ann's desk. "What are we going to do about this? She's really expecting a time machine."

"She does understand that the TARDIS is a television prop, surely?"

"She's mentioned the Great Glass Elevator."

"Great Glass Elevator?"

"Roald Dahl."

"Ah, yes, Wonka. But there's no need for a physical portal; a time machine is technically any means used to make time travel possible."

Beav removed his bandana and fiddled with it. "She won't be satisfied with that excuse."

Ann sighed. "It's not an excuse, it's how it is. All we need to make this possible is *her* – the data will be placed in her brain through a simple procedure that will take mere seconds. Activation requires only that she consciously choose to travel. It's highly intuitive."

Beav threw his hands up. "I know, I know. I don't want to be the one to tell her that there's no time machine. Can't we build her one?"

Ann smiled. "That's where I thought this was going." She grabbed another pencil and pointed the tip of it at Beav. "You'll have to be clever about it. If she suspects that the time machine is bogus our good deed will humiliate her."

Beav flashed a cocky grin. "Leave it to the techie gypsy. I'm going to build her a real time machine."

"Oh? And how will you manage that?"

"I'll program the machine to work as a power source, kind of. I think that's the way to go anyway. If she could travel without limitations using only her mind she could, and likely *would*, accidentally zip off to some other dimension while dreaming or letting her thoughts drift. In fact I've worried about such a scenario. I can't imagine adding the time space continuum as another place to go looking for her when she inevitably turns up missing at some point during the mission."

"I see your point and I raise you another. The data can be shared across more than one platform, correct? What I'm getting at is that I don't like the idea that Serena has to find her way back to the portal. Give her an emergency back-up."

Beav considered Ann's request before responding. "I could make a wristband for her, with the same basic functions as the time machine. I can pitch it to her as an 'emergency back-up'. I don't want her to know that the time machine is completely irrelevant."

"Agreed. This is a good idea all around. The time machine will have a true function and it will make Serena happy.

The wristband will give me peace of mind."

"Win-win."

Ann reached across the desk to shake Beav's hand. "I do like to win."

3

Mandolin Fredrik took the cash without counting it. He had reached a certain level at which he never needed to fear that someone would cheat him. If the numbers didn't add up his people would sort it out and his customers knew that. Most of his clients found a way to pay; it was either that or prepare an obituary for one of their family members, and then another and another until the bill was settled.

"It's all there."

"I know." Mandolin gave the man the once-over. "What I don't know is why you won't take care of this yourself. You don't look like you need someone to do your heavy lifting."

"You got your money. Do your job."

Mandolin raised his hands over his head in a "don't shoot" pantomime. "Hey, you don't want to tell me, I won't ask. But if you ever want a job, you look good for it."

Jorgi Gorantisch snorted, walked away, got into his car and drove off. Mandolin watched the car for a few seconds. Never had he done business with someone so physically intimidating. He tried to guess what would bring such a man to his services. He lingered in the truck stop parking lot, whistling and kicking small bits of gravel with his well-worn oxfords. As he turned to leave he noticed that his new client had company.

"Oh brother, what are you into?" Mandolin said aloud. He reached into his back pocket for his phone. His client's number was the last call received. "Hey, man, you've got a tail. Old school black Lexus. Yeah, no problem. Ring if you need…" Mandolin stared at the phone. He said aloud, even though he was speaking only to a dial tone, "No one cuts me off."

He returned his phone to his pocket and contemplated what he should do. He was due at his sister's place for his nephew's birthday party, but she'd get over it if he was late. He got into his car and started it up. It wouldn't delay him much if he followed his client's tail for a few minutes.

It wasn't difficult for him to make up for lost time on the road. He was soon a few feet behind the Lexus without anyone the wiser. He drove without incident for a good five miles before something interesting happened. His client took a frontage road, as did the Lexus and Mandolin. Mandolin watched as his client drove behind a home improvement store and the Lexus followed. *Well, well, what have we here?* Mandolin knew that his client wasn't so stupid as to lead his tail behind the store unless he planned to confront him---or work with him. What was going on?

Mandolin was now late for his nephew's party. The brightly wrapped birthday present on the passenger's seat reminded him of this when it slid, setting off electronic sound effects from the toy inside the box. He might as well go on to the party. He was done here anyway. If he followed them behind the store his cover would be blown. His client could take him;

44

that he knew, never mind that there were now at least two of them. And whatever was happening was none of his concern. He turned around and headed back to the frontage road. His decision was made: the less he knew the better. He had his money and a job to do. He would leave it at that.

Natalie Buske Thomas

4

Beav insisted that he be present when the tech crew introduced Serena to Ruby Red. In naming the time machine, all of the Gödel Solution Institute staff members were invited to put their name into a hat. Over a celebratory lunch, highlighted by coffee and cake, secretary Ruby's name was drawn— or at least it appeared to be drawn, she was approaching her seventy-fifth birthday and it was unanimously decided to give the prize to her. Ruby's reaction to this honor didn't disappoint. She had been none the wiser that the contest was rigged, as Serena was none the wiser that the time travel machine was artificially created just for her.

Building a portal wasn't as frivolous of an idea as it seemed on the surface; on closer inspection it made good sense. Beav was for the most part successful in convincing the crew that the time travel machine was a necessity. It was a valid concern that Serena wouldn't have been able to control the time travel switch. Her brain could have activated it without her intention, such as when she was sleeping.

Beav was less worried about Serena's nighttime dreams than he was about her wandering thoughts when she was wide awake. Regardless of how the mishap would have occurred, Beav was quite certain that a mishap most definitely would have occurred; it was only a matter of time. This was almost verbatim what Beav had pitched to the tech crew, but it didn't take much convincing to get people on board with the project. Most of them were more than eager to build the world's first real working time travel machine. One member said that a once-in-a-lifetime opportunity like this was why he became a scientist in the first place.

Ruby Red was, of course, red—a glorious shiny metallic red, like Serena's first car, long before the minivan had entered the scene. Beav had consulted Serena's husband Tom often during the designing of Ruby Red for insight into her favorite things. And the extremes he was willing to go to! He hadn't slept more than five or six odd hours all weekend, but it was all worth it; his busted thumb (he didn't look forward to when the nail would unavoidably fall off), his aching shoulders, his empty bank account (GSI didn't give him enough funding up front so he had to temporarily foot the bill from his own paycheck), and everything else he went through. He knew that he had achieved perfection when he saw the look on her face. *Yes*, he thought, *it was all worth it.*

"I don't know what to say." Serena clasped her hands together and her eyes shone with Christmas-morning glee. Her long dark hair was an unruly tangle and her short stature was made even shorter because she was wearing moccasins. These things added to her already childlike image. The Christmas-morning scene was complete when she jumped up and down, squealing, "I love it, I love it!"

The GSI scientists didn't know what to make of this unprofessional display, but most of them settled upon amusement. Serena bounced all around the perimeter of the time travel machine, occasionally stopping to admire the view. Finally she stood still. She touched the glossy finish, ran her hands over the smooth surface, and re-clasped her hands.

The time machine was shaped like an egg and stood six feet tall. Beav would have made the machine bigger but since Serena was barely over five feet tall, why not economize on the square footage? A bottomless budget was somewhat possible but it best not to be wasteful nonetheless.

The shiny red egg mesmerized Serena. She stared at the machine in silence for several seconds. Then she gasped, "I haven't even looked inside!"

Beav bowed and indicated the front of the machine with a flourish of sweeping gestures. "Step this way to embark upon Ruby Red."

"Ruby Red? Very nice." Serena found the door and stopped short. "How do I open it?"

"Mind control."

"What?" Serena looked more horrified than intrigued.

"Just kidding. There's a retina scanner under this panel. Show it one of your peepers and you're in."

The tech crew observed Serena's reaction to Ruby Red with as much pride as Beav had. There were fourteen members of the crew and all were in attendance. The most senior member, Buick—no one knew whether or not that was his real name—nudged Serena. "What are you waiting for?"

The crew crowded around the door. Serena showed her right eyeball to Ruby Red and was rewarded by a melodic tune: *I'm always chasing rainbows, Watching clouds drifting by.* "What song is this?"

Beav's confidence wavered. "It's a song called 'I'm Always Chasing Rainbows'. Judy Garland performed it, but most people only know her by that other rainbow song."

"I love it!" Serena grinned.

Beav leaned sideways to meet Buick's ear and whispered, "As long as she doesn't look up the rest of the lyrics we're good."

Serena peered through the door. "What other surprises do you have for me?"

Buick pressed in closer. "Go in and see for yourself!" He gave Beav a little shove to clear the way for him to create a video of Serena's entry into the time machine. This was not only a personal and professional achievement for GSI and its tech team, but a historic moment for the entire planet. Buick expected his video to go viral instantly.

Serena's initial reaction was to giggle. "I can't believe it! It's like all of my favorite things were brought in and crammed into this giant red egg!"

Beav spun around and gave the crew a thumb's up sign. The team cheered with catcalls, shouts, and applause. Only one crew member abstained from what he considered to be a ludicrous charade. He, Roger McCloy, was a technical scientist not a stage designer! To say that he wasn't impressed with Serena Wilcox would be an understatement. Inventing a time machine to accommodate her ignorance of time travel technology was senseless, but Roger's attitude didn't dampen the jubilant mood that the rest of them shared.

Serena examined everything while Buick captured every moment on video. The crew couldn't see much past Ruby Red's small doorway but Buick's camera was wirelessly connected to a large screen outside of the machine. The crew clustered around the screen to watch Serena's reaction to all of the many details that they had helped Beav bring to fruition. Crew members patted each other on the back as each of their areas of expertise were displayed and appreciated.

Serena hopped onto the black leather seat that was situated in the absolute middle of the egg's interior. She swung her feet, unable to touch the floor. Under the chair was a bed of flowers: daisies, lavender, black-eyed susans and four different varieties of roses; two red and two yellow. One of the red varieties was a climbing rose. Roses had been trained to grow up the sides of the egg's interior walls. Serena was encased in flowers.

She admired the flowers for much longer than the crew's patience could bear. Finally Buick called out, "Look at the control panel!"

Beav shushed him, "Give her time, give her time."

Serena moved beyond the flowers and took in the rest of Ruby Red's environment. She noticed a drop-down screen with pre-loaded movies, television shows, and music built into the panel. "When will I have time for all of this? Isn't time travel instant?"

Beav explained. "That's only in case of unforeseen delays, so you'll have something to entertain yourself with." His private thoughts were *so you stay out of trouble until we reach you.*

Serena sighed with relief. "You had me thinking that you were sending me off on a long flight. I hate to fly."

Roger McCloy piped up; quick to illustrate how right he was when objecting to this project. "You hate to fly? Then what's this nonsense been about?"

Beav scowled at him. "Disregard anything he says, Serena. Yes, you'll be instantly transported either to the past or to the future."

"Good. I'm also claustrophobic. I won't like it when the door closes."

"What the…" Roger's sentence was cut off by Beav's hand clamping over his mouth.

Beav reassured her. "Again, no worries. You won't be in there long. But tell me, what do you think now that you've seen the inside?"

Serena continued to look around. "I love it! I love the flowers, the entertainment system, and the makeup mirror is a nice touch too."

"Make up mirror?" Beav was confused.

Roger sniggered. "The control panel. This chick couldn't be more clueless if she were blonde."

"Hey, misogynist—shut up. In fact, I'm done with you." Beav told Buick to stop filming. "Get him off the team. We can't keep anyone who doesn't respect Serena Wilcox."

Buick sputtered, "You're serious?"

Serena's voice sounded far away from inside the machine. "I don't want to get anyone fired."

Beav nodded to Buick. "Get him out *now*." To Serena he said, "It's not up to you. They've put me in charge of Project Scarecrow, so I'm... Well, you work for me. I know you're used to it being, uh, the other way around."

The light dawned slowly. "Oh, I see. Beav, I couldn't ask for a better person to work for. I have to ask though, how does Agent Estep play into this? Why hasn't he graced us with his presence?"

Beav shrugged. "I'm not sure why he's not here. Estep is running the operation from a tactical standpoint. If you ask him, he'll say he's the man in charge. But I'm the guy who will get you home safe.

Speaking of, I want you to wear this at all times."

Serena said, "I heard what you said, but barely. It's hard to hear anything from inside here."

Beav reached into the machine and snapped the wristband on Serena's wrist. "I said 'I want you to wear this at all times'. It's your emergency back-up. If you lose your way back to the portal you can use this. It has the same basic keypad that Ruby Red has."

"What keypad? It's obvious where it is on the bracelet but I don't see any keypad in here."

Buick had passed Roger's walk-out duty on to Jorgi to deal with and was already back at his post, video-taping Serena's responses to Ruby Red. He said, "The keypad is in the control panel."

"How do I... Oh, I see." She waved her hand in front of the mirror and it popped open, revealing a dazzling array of lights. "Ah, the keypad, and so much more!" She found the button labeled *intercom*. She pressed it. "Say something."

Serena's voice was amplified through Ruby Red's exterior speakers. The crew shouted in unison, "Something!"

Serena held her hands over her ears. "Wow! I'll have to adjust the volume. You guys about blew my eardrums out."

Beav laughed. "Do you feel better about the sound issue?"

"Oh yes. This machine is amazing! Is there anything that it *can't* do?"

Beav mulled it over. "There are some obvious ways it will fail you. There's no, um, restroom, so eventually you'll be in trouble if you are stuck in there too long, which is why we won't let that happen. Also, if you check the control panel you'll find a few meal bars. There's no water, except for what's bottled and stored in the cube locker on your right. If trapped in there too long you'll run out of food and water, but not for several days-- weeks even, if you ration. The restroom issue will be the worst of your problems in the short term. I mean, *would* be the worst. We won't let you get stuck in there."

An awkward silence fell as everyone wondered if Beav's pledge was a bad omen. Also, the reality that Roger McCloy had just been fired was sinking in through the feel-good emotions that had initially steered the group's chemistry. Most of all, the fatigue caused by their all-nighters was hitting them now that the adrenaline rush was over.

Serena attempted to shrug off their collective funk. "I have the back-up bracelet, what could go wrong?" No one said anything. Serena prattled on. "The skylight is a nice touch. Well done everybody! I'm proud to be your first time traveler."

The crew murmured their appreciation of her compliments. Serena hopped off the chair, taking care not to catch the heel of her foot on the flower bed planter edging. She took one final look around before exiting the egg.

Malirah and Jo met Serena as she stepped out. Malirah's smooth chocolate skin couldn't have made a more striking contrast to Jo's fair Irish complexion. Both women were slender and young, with a bright perky look in their eyes. They were equal parts stunning and intimidating. Serena felt as if Malirah and Jo were warrior princesses from another planet and she was perhaps their troll sidekick.

Malirah had been hiding something behind her back. She revealed it now. "You aren't finished yet. Try this on."

Serena reached out for the pilot's hat that Malirah offered her. It was a perfect fit.

Malirah laughed. "Better you than me. I don't do 'hat head'." She pointed to her afro halo which was highlighted today by an ornate jeweled hairpiece.

Jo reminded Malirah to give Serena the emerald scarf. "That was my pick. I remembered that your eyes are green."

Serena laughed. "And I remember that I glommed onto your Irish roots, hoping to find a connection to my own. You were quick to mention that with all the Murphys there are in Ireland we probably aren't cousins."

"Did you ever find your Murphy line?" Jo asked.

"Not yet." Serena froze when she realized that Malirah was waiting to adorn her with the green scarf.

Malirah, who was already nearly six feet tall when flat-footed, stooped over from her perch on her six-inch gold boots. She arranged the scarf around Serena's neck, fussing with it as if Serena was a dress-up doll.

Serena ran her hands admiringly over both the pilot's hat and the scarf. Next she let her eyes rest upon the onyx and silver high-tech bracelet on her left wrist. She breathed in and out slowly and deeply. She knew what would make this day complete. "Someone mentioned a red velvet cake with non-dairy whipped topping. Would you happen to have any of that left?"

5

Mandolin was waiting for Roger McCloy to arrive at his home at the end of a quiet cul-de-sac of a prominent subdivision. Roger pulled into his driveway and almost made it into his garage before he noticed that Mandolin was standing in front of it. He stopped the car and opened the driver's side window. "Can I help you?"

Mandolin leaned into the window and, faster than Roger could respond, reached through it to shut off the ignition. "Yes, you can."

Something about the hard look in Mandolin's eyes made Roger understand the gravity of the situation. "Hey, whatever it is that you want, can this wait? I'll give you my number and we can talk later." Mandolin slowly shook his head. "Then tell me what you want, but I'm not getting out of the car with you standing there threatening me."

Mandolin reached through the window for a second time. With his right hand popping through first, he grabbed Roger by the collar. Next he reached in with his left hand and opened the car door. He pulled Roger out as if saving him from a burning vehicle. He released him onto the ground with unnecessary force.

Roger popped back up like a clown in a Jack-in-a-box. "Point taken. I'll do whatever you say, for now. My wife's home. She'll look out eventually and call the police." Roger was much slimmer than Mandolin and he had no experience with self-defense of any kind. He hadn't even been able to hold his own against his younger sister.

Mandolin was expressionless and toneless when he said, "I have two words for you: Disgruntled Employee."

Roger stared at him. "I was fired today. What do you know about it?"

Mandolin invaded Roger's personal space. "You can tell me what you know about the Gödel Solution Institute."

"Whoa!" Roger waved his arms and took a step backward. "Espionage? No way. I'm a scientist. I got fired because I wouldn't bend my ethics. Why would I bend them now?"

"Ethics? Is that what you call sexual harassment?" Mandolin sniggered. "You're a little weasel, aren't you?"

"Sexual harassment? Is that what they're saying? It's a mockery of our work to create a façade. There's no logic behind turning technology into cosmetology; it's a farce and a blatant disregard for anything resembling an adult working environment. That woman doesn't live in the real world and lacks the intelligence to comprehend the project. If scientific integrity is sexual harassment I'm better off without that place."

"Look, Weasel, I don't like pencil necks like you. We aren't going to be friends. But you *are* going to tell me about the Gödel Solution Institute."

"My wife…"

"Save your breath. Your wife isn't coming out."

Roger's eyes widened. "What did you do to her?"

Mandolin held up his hand. "Relax, she's fine. My associate is watching over her. Let's go in now, shall we?"

Roger's shoulders slumped but he complied. He even held the door open for Mandolin to enter his home through the front door foyer entrance. Although he held onto the faint hope that his neighbors had noticed something suspicious and phoned it in, he knew that he had burned too many bridges to realistically expect anyone to care what was happening at the McCloy abode. If anything, his neighbors were relishing his discomfort.

Roger knew he wasn't likely to make good on a resolution to become a better person when all of this was all said and done. But if he came out of this alive, Roger vowed that he would dial back on his tendency to shoot his mouth off, something his wife had been begging him to do for years. Roger followed Mandolin into the living room.

Mandolin didn't wait for an invitation. He dropped his bulk onto a leather sofa. He surveyed the original oil paintings on the walls, the art deco lamps, the bookshelf loaded with books that he suspected were never opened, and the high-end entertainment center with all of the latest bells and whistles. Mandolin observed, "Science must pay well."

Roger scowled. "It *did*."

Mandolin rubbed his hands together and echoed, "It *did*."

Roger sat in the recliner and then resumed standing when he was too keyed up to sit.

"You're going to need money." Mandolin emphasized.

"Stop toying with me. I know what you're doing. How much are you offering

70

and what do you want to know? Who wants to know it? Why do they want to know it? Why should I throw my career overboard for this? I can get hired somewhere else."

Mandolin raised his eyebrows. "Are you finished?"

Roger put his hands in his pockets and paced the room. "I'm finished."

"We don't care about your science. All we want are a few details about personnel. If I were you, I'd be licking my boots right about now. Take the handout. I won't be back with another offer."

Roger perked up. "Personnel? What personnel? I'll gladly throw someone under the bus."

Mandolin snorted. "I figured you had an axe to grind. Tell me what you know about Eduardo."

"Eduardo?"

"Your boss. You know him."

71

"Yeah, but, what do you want to know about him? He's a Boy Scout."

Mandolin rolled his eyes.

Roger sat in the recliner. "He's not?"

Mandolin laughed. "Weasel, get your head out of your skinny behind. No one's a Boy Scout."

Roger's eyes narrowed. "Who are you?"

Mandolin shook his head. "You don't need to know. Tell me about Eduardo."

Roger shrugged. "I don't know much about him. We didn't exactly hang out."

"Tell me what he does for GSI."

"I don't know."

Mandolin leapt off the couch and reared up to his full height like a grizzly bear on the attack. "You're lying!"

Roger couldn't move or speak.

"Do we need to get your wife to make a little noise?" Mandolin shouted at the ceiling. "Make her scream."

A hideous shriek rang through their ears. The sound carried on for two or three seconds then suddenly stopped.

"No! No! Leave her alone!" Roger was on his feet and had jumped onto the recliner. He tilted his head toward the ceiling and yelled, "I'll talk! Don't hurt her!"

Mandolin sat back down and gestured for Roger to do the same. Both men sat. Roger sighed. "What do you want to know?"

Natalie Buske Thomas

6

Serena held the card that her husband and kids had signed for her big launch day tightly with both hands. It was the one thing she had remembered to bring with her. She had forgotten her emergency inhaler, should she have a rare but nerve-wracking asthma attack, her phone, which she finally did commit to buying but had now left at home, and the travel instruction list she'd made. All of this was in her purse that was sitting on her kitchen counter.

A flash of movement caught her eye. She looked past the crew huddled around Ruby Red and saw a face that belonged to her. She surprised herself by tearing up a little. "Tom? I thought you couldn't make it?"

"I can't stay. I just dropped by to give you this." He held out her purse, containing her inhaler, her phone, her travel instructions and miscellaneous other items of varying usefulness.

Serena grasped the purse and held the strap for a bit longer than necessary. Tom gave her a quizzical look. She replied with a hug. He spoke into her ear, "You'll be fine."

The couple released their embrace, Tom left, and the crew bustled around the exterior of the time machine. Serena paced. She idly watched the crew until she realized that she knew little about these people. She upped her observations to the intensity of a conscious assessment.

She started with the two most memorable crew members: Malirah Cravitz and honorary (non-technical) member Jo. Both were sharp, talented and strong women. Both had credentials out the wazoo. Both had natural charisma and an intimidating presence, but were most of all likeable and genuine. There was nothing about either woman that contradicted the image of a successful modern highly-educated fast-tracked young single female in a male-dominated industry. They were both movie-star good looking and nearly plastic in their perfection.

Serena chalked it up as highly unlikely that these two dynamic and dramatic center-of-attention high-profile women could be successful at keeping secrets if they wanted to. Jo had even dated the

President of the United States, Joseph Smythe. No one knew if Jo and Joe, as Serena had routinely called him before he took office (during their work together for Operation Covert Coffee), were seeing each other again, but there had been whispers about a certain redhead who had recently returned to the States from Ireland. It was only a matter of time before the whole world knew everything about Jo, right down to what perfume she wore (none, but she smelled like strawberry shampoo) and what she had for lunch (usually a grilled chicken salad).

Having been sucked into the political quagmire until she had nearly lost her life, Serena wasn't eager to know anything relating to politics, the new administration, or the new President, no matter how likeable Joe was, but she would hear all about it eventually. Serena dismissed both Malirah and Jo as potential threats, not that

Edison. Serena had met the three several times, but she didn't have a pulse on any of them.

She studied them now. They were all pre-occupied with final adjustments; to what, she didn't know, but their preoccupation allowed her to evaluate and profile them without their awareness. She began with Jorgi. He looked like a bouncer, not a scientist. The remaining two men were nondescript and average looking in every way. It was hard for Serena to remember which man was Gentry and which man was James Edison.

At that moment someone opened the door to Ruby Red. It was time for one last check of the control panel. One by one they leaned in, gasped, and pulled back as if stung.

Serena stepped in to see what all the fuss was about. In a grotesque position, slumped over Ruby Red's glorious flower

81

bed planter, was a member of the crew that Serena had only just realized was missing. "Poor Gentry," she said. Then she turned to Beav and whispered, "Or is that James Edison?"

The man's identity was confirmed when Malirah rushed forward and screamed, "Gentry!" Her manicured nails didn't stand in the way of her being the first to reach in for her fallen comrade. She shrieked, "Help me get him out of there!"

Agent Estep and former agent Lehman intervened. Lehman pulled Malirah away from Ruby Red's small door. Estep held his hands up in a crowd-control gesture. "We have to treat this as a crime scene."

Malirah strained against Lehman's hold. "No! Help him, help him!"

Jo and Dr. Kendra slipped into crisis intervention roles. Each of them eased Malirah into the reality that Gentry was long dead. He had been dead for at least twenty-four hours, by rough first-glance estimate. They'd know more later.

Serena stated the obvious. "We'll have to postpone the launch."

"Your deductive reasoning is as astute as ever, Ms. Wilcox," Estep grumbled, his voice dripping with sarcastic inflection. "Do whatever it is you do, *over there*, with them." He pointed to the crew who had assembled in a shell-shocked clutch.

Serena saluted, ignored Estep's grimace, and ushered the clutch of crew members into GSI's generous lobby. Standing tall at barely over five-feet-one, the group swallowed Serena whole. She instructed them to sit. The balance of power shifted in her favor. She began.

"It looks like I'll be in my familiar role of investigating crimes that are happening in real time, sadly no time machine required." Serena gauged their facial reactions. So far she saw nothing unexpected in any of them.

The man she now knew through process of elimination to be James Edison said, "Am I to assume that you're starting with us?"

Serena touched the side of her nose as in a game of charades—*bingo*. "This should go fast. There are only six of you. We have three women; Kendra, Jo, and Malirah. And we have three men; Jorgi, James Edison, and Eduardo. There's a fourth if Roger returned to GSI after he was fired. We'll check that out."

Kendra raised her hand, waited for Serena to acknowledge her, and then said, "I was at a conference in Orlando. I flew back this morning and came straight here from the airport."

"Do you have any insight into the relationships between the crew members, or anything else to share?" Serena asked this as a formality, but she knew that Kendra had even less contact with the crew than she did. As expected, Kendra shook her head. "You're free to go."

Kendra didn't hesitate.

"And then there were five," said Malirah.

"Did you know Gentry intimately?" Serena searched Malirah's face for telltale micro-expressions. She saw amusement.

"Intimately? As in, were we lovers?" Malirah laughed. "I think he may have lived in his parents' basement. No, we were definitely not lovers. I'm just freaking out because he's *dead*. I've never seen a dead person before, and he's someone I knew. I worked with him. He's dead. I can't believe he's right out there, all... dead."

Jo added, "I've been in Ireland most of the past year but even I know that

Malirah is engaged to a football player. How did you miss seeing her face on the tabloid covers every week?"

Serena pressed on. "Malirah, where were you the past couple of days?"

"Home, here. Home, here. The usual." Malirah stood up. "Can I go? I'm feeling nauseous. You might be used to seeing dead people, but I'm not."

Serena waved her off. "Yes, go ahead. Jo, you can go too."

Jorgi snorted. "You don't think women can kill people?"

Serena's eyes narrowed. She said, her voice barely audible, "*I've* killed people."

Eduardo sputtered and choked.

She said, "I'm not proud of it. It was kind of a wrong time, wrong place situation. It wasn't exactly my fault, any of the times."

Eduardo sputtered and choked again. "You've killed multiple times?"

Serena addressed Jorgi. "I'm done with those three because they're innocent, not because they're women. I'm keeping you three here because you could be guilty, not because you're men."

"What!" James Edison popped up out of his seat. "Hey, I don't know anything. Gentry is— *was* — my friend. All I know is that he was alive yesterday and now he's dead."

Serena perked up. "When do you last see him?"

James Edison bit his lower lip. "I don't know. I can't remember." He sat back down. "Wait. I do remember. He said he was going to be late if he didn't leave right now. It takes him fifteen minutes, depending on traffic, to get there. So to get there on time, he'd have to leave by 5:45."

Serena did the mental math. "He had a 6:00 appointment? Where?"

James Edison was staring at his hands. He looked up, surprised. "He was on dialysis. Everyone knew that. He had a standard appointment."

"Doesn't dialysis take about four hours? His appointment would have kept him there until ten o'clock. I can't imagine a facility open that late."

"I'm not sure when the dialysis unit closes. I think they may actually keep late hours, but anyway, I know his treatments didn't take as long as four hours. He did high-flux dialysis, or something like that. He must have left here around 5:45 and he was headed to his treatment. That's all I know."

Serena switched gears. "Was Malirah being impish or did Gentry live with his parents?"

James Edison stood back up. "He lived at home, yes. He was a good man and my friend. He helped take care of his parents, and they helped take care of him. Everyone in that house had multiple medical problems. Malirah's drama about seeing dead people aside, she knew nothing about Gentry, and didn't care to. Gentry was my friend. If anyone should be shaken up, it's me. Unless you have any real reason to keep me, I'm leaving now."

Serena offered James Edison a hug, which he rejected. "I'm truly sorry for your loss," she said. She released him, which left her with only two: Jorgi and Eduardo.

Jorgi scoffed. "This is going nowhere. I'm out of here."

"No you're not. I ruled James Edison out, but the two of you are guilty." Serena anticipated that the reaction to her accusation might be dicey. She placed her hand into the side pocket of the purse that her husband Tom had dropped off to her earlier. She grabbed hold of one of its most important contents: a mini tranquilizer gun.

Because the gun was a licensed government-issue weapon, it had required an exemption from the civil service requirement. The only way to get that exemption was by taking a gun safety course, and by obtaining a waiver signed by Agent Estep. Estep's signature was barely dry on the waiver that had been turned in only yesterday.

Sure enough, Serena's gut feeling was correct. She had a reason to shoot the gun outside of the range. Serena prided herself on her beginner's luck when the darts hit her intended target with remarkable precision. She admired her work for a second before notifying Estep.

7

Agent Estep stood facing Serena, hands on his hips, chest puffed out as if he was brandishing a sheriff's badge. "Explain."

Serena shrugged. "What's to explain? Jorgi made a move and I shot him with the tranquilizer gun."

"Made a move to do what? How is it that we have one dead person already and now you've made this mess? It's déjà vu all over again."

Beav quipped, "You said 'already seen' when you said 'déjà vu'. When you added 'all over again' you made yourself redundant."

Estep ignored him. "I'm not the only one who sees this ongoing pattern with Serena Wilcox, dead people, and something to clean up."

Beav pushed his luck. "Again, redundant; 'ongoing' and 'pattern'. You implied that something ongoing produces a pattern. You don't need both."

Estep snarled. "Shut up and get me some coffee."

Beav snickered. "Just yanking your chain. And, no, I'm not getting you coffee."

Serena interrupted. "Guys, he's starting to come to."

Jorgi stirred, raised himself up on his elbows, opened one eye, and then flopped back into a prone position. Estep, Beav and Lehman watched him. Satisfied that he was immobile for the time being, Lehman snapped his fingers to get Estep's attention. "You have any cuffs on you?"

Estep tossed a set of handcuffs on the floor. Beav kicked them with his foot. The cuffs slid into place where Lehman was kneeling by Jorgi. Two clicks later and Jorgi's captivity was confirmed. Serena was impressed. "Wow, how long did it take the three of you to choreograph that? We should set it to music next time."

Estep let that go. "You never did say. What move was Jorgi making? Why is he the suspect?"

Serena pointed at Eduardo. "He's involved too."

Beav whistled. "I thought the twofer was accidental, or incidental."

93

Eduardo had been knocked out cold by the weight of Jorgi's grizzly-bear form falling on top of him. He was currently still pinned under the now-cuffed Jorgi. Lehman hadn't bothered to roll Jorgi off of him. The four of them looked down at the unlikely pair. Jorgi's massive body almost blotted Eduardo's out completely. It was like a macabre ventriloquism act in which both puppeteer and puppet were silenced in one fell swoop.

Lehman glanced at Estep. "I don't suppose you have another set of those?"

Estep shook his head. "That little guy isn't going anywhere."

Serena sighed. "I suppose I should have called you in sooner, but I didn't know for sure that these two were involved until I pushed them and they reacted. I doubt I could have gotten that response if I wasn't alone with them. It was only because Jorgi didn't see me as a threat that he tried that stunt. If you'd been there he would have hedged his bets differently, denying everything to the end."

Beav prompted her. "Tried what? He went after you?"

"No, no. He went after Eduardo. He would have killed him if I hadn't shot him. He was well on his way to snapping his neck."

Lehman held up both hands. "Back up. This is getting complicated. I promised my wife that I'm only here as a consult. Don't say anything more until I'm out of the room; if I don't know anything I can't be involved."

Beav clapped Lehman on the back, "Sorry, you're already involved. Pull up a seat. Ann Kinji will want to see all of our faces when she gets here."

Serena's mouth twisted into a lopsided clown-faced frown. "You already called her?"

Beav glared at Estep. "*He* did. And I see he must have called in some friends too."

Crime scene investigators and police officers took over the premises while an ambulance transported both men to the nearest hospital. There was nothing left for the four of them to do but sit in Ann Kinji's empty office and wait for her to arrive.

Everyone but Beav sat. He, for reasons known only to him, made enough coffee for a banquet full of people, even though he wouldn't drink a drop of it himself. His strict code of fitness and a personal distaste for coffee meant that he nearly always abstained from the caffeine drip that the others so desperately sought.

He served Estep and said, "Don't get used to it. I'm only doing this once."

Estep, Lehman and Serena sipped their coffee and reflected upon the day's events. Serena broke the silence. "So, how's everyone been?"

Estep snorted.

Lehman said, "I can't complain. Life's been good to me. I'm blessed. And, I'd like to keep it that way. I'm only staying on until you get your communications worked out. Then I'm turning the reigns over to your new IT guy, or gal."

Serena glossed over everything he said. "Are you still in Texas?"

"Yes, I'm still in Texas. Except that I'm *not* in Texas. My wife is sitting by our pool alone, with no one manning the grill."

Serena gave up. "How about you, Beav? Anything new?"

Beav clucked his tongue. "You've seen me every day. This is my life now. We're putting you in a time machine. What more could there be?"

"Oh for the love of…When is Kinji getting here?" Estep's patience, always on low ebb, had worn out.

Serena never left well enough alone. "So, Estep, how about you? How's your dog Finn doing? Did I hear that you and Katarina got back together?"

Estep bolted, slamming the door behind him. He came back in two seconds later, red-faced, with Ann on his heels.

Giggles surfaced but Ann shut that down with one look. The speed in which she had entered the office had started her famous bob swinging. Even the locks of her hair had the power to take command of a room.

Without any further prompting Lehman summarized, "Crew member Gentry Davis was found dead inside the time machine. We secured the crime scene and Serena interviewed the remaining crew. Of these she released all but the two suspects, Jorgi Gorantisch and Eduardo Martin."

"Corruption from within, why am I not surprised?" Ann grabbed a pencil off her desk, but stopped herself before she gnawed the eraser. She sat, tapped the pencil on the lip of the desk, and fumed. "We've seen this before. It's déjà vu all over again."

Everyone looked at Beav, begging him with their eyes not to correct Ann's misuse of "déjà vu". He said, "Yeah, what she said." Then, at a level that only Serena could hear, he couldn't resist adding, "Redundantly."

Ann continued, "Does this have anything to do with my mysterious ex-convicts at the gala?"

Serena nodded. "Absolutely."

Beav, Estep and Lehman stared at her. Beav said, "What? How do you know this?"

Serena was tempted to tease them with a story about how she deduced this after following a complex series of clues, but she couldn't come up with brilliant fiction fast enough. She settled on the truth. "Just before Jorgi tried to strangle Eduardo he said, 'I'm not going back inside because of you.'"

Ann frowned. "I would have recognized Jorgi if he'd been at the gala. Those were friends of his?"

Serena nodded. "I'm assuming that's what will check out. As soon as either of them is cleared by the hospital for interrogation, we'll definitely be on it." Serena said this as if she was creating a plan for all of them to follow.

Ann left her office without replying, and without any explanation about where she was going or if she would be returning. No one thought anything of this, as she was well known for her sudden departures—and sudden arrivals, as Estep had just experienced. They knew better than to say anything that they didn't want her to overhear. And yet, as soon as she left the room they couldn't resist the urge to speak candidly.

Estep was noticeably perturbed by Serena's sudden power grab, a grab that Serena wasn't even aware that she was making. He said, "Hold up. I'm taking lead on this. You stay here and do whatever it is that you do."

Lehman groaned. "Look, this isn't happening—the typical tit for tat bickering and nonsense. I'm going to take the next flight out of here if you don't get your act together. I'm tired. I'm sick of kids running past my hotel room door, waking me up every night. I'm done with this weather. I'm done with restaurant food. Give me one more reason to leave and you'll have to finish this without your IT consult."

Serena squeezed his arm. "Please stay on. In a few more days we'll be back on track and you'll be home by the end of the month."

"Last time I worked with you I got strapped to explosives and knocked unconscious."

Estep protested. "We aren't responsible for that, and you're fine. Nothing bad came of it. But if you want out, you're a civilian. I have no authority over you."

Beav laughed.

Estep spun around to face him. "What's so funny?"

Beav tipped his head toward Serena. "You forgot who was listening."

Serena smiled broadly. "Did I hear you say, my dear Agent Estep, that you have no authority over civilians?"

Lehman put his arms around Estep and Serena. "So it's the two of you who are running down the hall waking me up every night?"

Estep brushed Lehman's arm off his shoulders. "We're getting testy, I admit it. What did you expect? Launch day was a disaster: one man down and two more in custody. The tally is three crew members gone. Project Scarecrow couldn't have gone worse."

Beav disagreed. "It *can* be worse. If Eduardo is in cahoots with Jorgi we're in big trouble. Eduardo is the lead scientist for Project Scarecrow. They could have sabotaged the project or sold our secrets."

"Who's saying that they haven't already?" Serena was quick to point out.

Lehman asked, "What project, what secrets, and who are 'they'? I've been doing my part without seeing much of how the pieces come together. I should have asked more questions, but I was confident that I didn't want to know the answers."

Serena prodded. "Are you sure you want to know the answers *now*?"

"No, but I need to know what I'm involved in."

Beav accommodated. "Here's what we know: Project Scarecrow was named as such because the Scarecrow only needed a brain. It's an Oz reference, you know, Frank Baum, Wizard of Oz?"

Estep grumbled. "He gets it."

Serena took over. "Scientists discovered how to access data stored in the human brain. They need the right brains though, from people who have been alive, or will be alive, during the points in the past or future that they want access to. That's how the time travel technology works. They can convert data from the human brain into digital information. I'm simplifying this. I haven't seen the old time machine, the one they used before Ruby Red, so I don't know how they were traveling before now, but time travel has already been done, and there's concern that the technology has already been abused, almost before the technology was even discovered. Furthermore, there's potential that the technology will be, or has already been, sold to parties who intend to use the science for their own gain, with devastating negative repercussions. We don't actually know who 'they' are or what they are up to, but we know that there is a 'they'."

Estep said, "What old time machine? They didn't…"

Ann came up from behind them with the stealth of a panther, a formidable skill that her tiny Japanese-American frame was especially well suited for. She called out, "I'm glad you're still here. Eduardo is awake and ready for visitors. I had him transferred here. He's arriving in ten minutes."

8

J orgi Gorantisch knew that he should have been closely monitored, and allowed no outside communication. He chuckled to himself, knowing how livid former President Ann Kinji would be if she knew how easy it had been for him to make the call. Kinji's team would take the heat for this, as they should. Her people were so slow to arrive at the hospital that he had had plenty of time to put his next move into motion. He didn't fault the hospital's security. He was, after all, in cuffs. Apparently they figured that he couldn't do any harm if he wasn't able to leave his bed.

Jorgi's disgust flared up as acid reflux. Security breaches at this level? This was exactly the sort of thing that motivated him to work for the other side. Once again the Americans had proven that they weren't competent enough to guard and protect the world's most significant and powerful technology. If Jorgi could hijack The Gödel Solution Institute so easily, anyone could. And that was his whole point. His cause was just: the world needed security and he was the man to prove it.

Jorgi knew he'd be branded as a traitor, but he cared little about what anyone thought. His loyalty was global, not national. Lest they forget, time travel technology didn't originate with Americans alone. What did they think would happen when they screwed up? Too many nations had a vested interest to simply walk away and let the institute fumble the ball. To be fair, he amended, they hadn't actually fumbled yet, this was more of a pre-emptive strike to prove that they could--- and would--fumble. Of course he spoke only for his own motivations. What the people above him wanted was unknown to him.

Jorgi had reached Mandolin on the first ring. Having plucked Mandolin's name nearly at random when trolling for ex-cons that he could leverage into service, Jorgi hadn't expected much, but Mandolin had proven to be a valuable asset. He understood what needed to be done and was there in person to do the job himself in less than ten minutes.

Mandolin, in custodian garb, was in and out of the hospital before Kinji's team had arrived on the scene. Jorgi smirked as he watched her team scratch their heads. Where oh where was their man Eduardo? Missing? How could it be?

Jorgi re-played the memory of Kinji's people stumbling around dazed and confused, then picking up the pace to a brisk walk, and then finally disintegrating into a mad scramble as their security detail ran every which way. The scene reminded him of the ant hills he delighted in crushing with his fist when he was a small child; ants scattering, scrambling over each other, frantic and brainless without their queen to guide them. And just like with the ants, all of that scrambling didn't change a thing.

Jorgi's amusement lasted well into the evening, making his last evening in the hospital almost a joy. He knew that he was headed back to prison, most likely a maximum security penitentiary this time around. He wouldn't let it get to him though. He had friends in much higher places than he did before. He anticipated that he'd be out within the year; with his record expunged, money in the bank, and a nice island to retire to. No, he wasn't sweating this.

That's why he never saw it coming when someone slipped something into his plastic tumbler of water. He didn't suspect anything even when he felt unusually and suddenly drowsy. He was still smug about the Gödel Solution Institute's security snafu as he slipped into a coma and flat-lined.

Natalie Buske Thomas

9

Ann Kinji stormed the halls of the Gödel Solution Institute while Estep's pager went bezerk from its perch on the granite countertop in the lobby. She asked, with no expectation of a response, "Why didn't he take that blasted thing with him?"

Serena picked up the pager and fumbled with it. She flipped it over and back again several times, clicking the button, thumping on it and flipping it back

113

and forth yet again. Lehman took the gadget from her, turned it off, and placed it back in her hand.

Serena slipped the pager into her purse with a mental note to return it to Estep when she next saw him, all the while knowing that the likelihood of him seeing his pager again anytime soon was practically nil.

Ann stopped moving long enough to engage Beav in strategic planning. "Can you imagine the PR nightmare that this has caused? Fortunately few know about this farce and it's not too late to bury it. Everything we do here is sanctioned by the United States government and I can sweep things under clearances so secret that not even I will be able to find the secrets I bury. Sometimes I think I have more power as President and CEO of the Gödel Solution Institute than I did when I was President of the United States. GSI is a hybrid of private sector and federal. It's complicated, it's new, and it's outside the law. It's my baby."

Beav, Lehman and Serena didn't know what to say when Ann wrestled with her conscience, so they wisely said nothing. They waited.

Ann resumed. "I can't let this fall apart. The institute is much bigger than you and me. This crisis we're dealing with now is in comparison no larger than a mite. We can't let it take down a project that could impact the entire world."

Beav felt prompted. "What do you want us to do?"

Ann answered him immediately, leaving them to wonder if she had prepared her response in advance or if she was thinking on her feet with lightning speed. Either scenario was equally plausible. "I want you to re-schedule the launch for as soon as possible: Tomorrow.

The Social Media Channel has been parroting this morning's cancelation all day, describing it as a 'technical difficulty'. If we jump back into the game soon enough GSI will be back on track without as much as a ding on her fender."

Beav assured her, "Yes, we can make that happen. The three missing crew members were part of the invention phase. We don't need them for the launch. We don't need them at all really. We'll do better with a smaller crew that we can more easily keep an eye on."

Ann considered this. "Estep will need to bring in additional agents from time to time to fill in the gaps. The director has given me a blank check so that's not a problem. I agree—keep our crew small."

She walked over to Lehman, where he was seated in an oversized chair directly across from her desk. "Any chance I can convince you to do some digging, a little light investigative work? Virtual work only, your area of expertise. You won't have to leave my office. I have everything you need right here." She indicated the wall of computers, surveillance cameras, and monitors.

"Of course. I'd be glad to help. I can stay on as long as you need me." Beav and Serena's heads flipped toward Lehman in stunned whiplash. He held up his index finger in a "wait one minute" sign. "But you know that I can do this just as easily from my house in Texas. Just shoot me the data and I'll work it through."

Ann stared at him. "You're kidding, right? I'm not transmitting anything to you. Nothing leaves this office. Besides, time is of the essence. I can't wait until you fly home and get set up on the other end. You need to start right now."

Lehman's jaw dropped open slightly. "I'm getting the impression that this isn't exactly a request."

Ann placed both palms flat on her desktop, distributed her weight onto her hands and rocked her forearms so that her upper body invaded Lehman's personal space. While Ann was small enough for Lehman to easily hoist her over his shoulders and carry her away, with her signature ebony bob swinging and her tiny feet no doubt kicking, her charisma was bigger than the pair of them combined. Lehman retreated as if confronted by a pit bull. Ann locked eyes with him and said, "I can't make you stay."

No one breathed until Lehman did. "Then it will be my pleasure to *choose* to stay." He realized that he meant it too. He couldn't realistically let go of this anyway--- he was already sucked in. Besides, he had the most understanding wife a man could wish for. He knew what she would say: Lehman was available for as long as they needed him. In his wife's eyes, Lehman was *the* hero, her hero. He had to admit that he rather liked that image. His shoulders slumped.

Beav and Serena watched Lehman's attitude transform live before their eyes in the space of about thirty seconds. Ann Kinji had that effect on people. It was a super power that never failed to impress them.

Ann sank into her chair and then turned her bird-like attention to Beav and Serena. "There's nothing more you can do that can't be done by Estep and his team. Eduardo is still missing and I'm not optimistic that we'll find him anytime soon. Wherever he is, he's long gone and it'll take the team at least until the end of the week to find him, that's my guess anyway. Jorgi is dead, so there's no hope in ever interrogating him. Lehman here will look into our own records, as he graciously volunteered to do. You two might as well go home and get some sleep. I need Serena to suit up tomorrow."

Beav and Serena stood up, both casting apologetic glances at Lehman, who they'd promised wouldn't be sucked in. They walked toward the door with halting steps, not sure if Ann expected them to say something. Beav was out the door first. Serena stopped in the doorway to add, "Project Scarecrow must go on. To infinity and--- " Beav pulled her out of the office before she could finish the line.

10

Ann Kinji had denied the media their many requests for press passes to yesterday's launch date. But Ann was singing a different tune today; she had flung the doors wide open for every journalist who could hitch a ride to the party, and she had even opened the event to the public. Project Scarecrow had evolved far from its original secrecy when it had become obvious that the project had been compromised.

What was a guarded and closed event just yesterday had today become an event so heavily populated that a crowd control swat team had been requested. The official explanation for the need for a swat team was that it was required solely as a precautionary measure due to the large numbers of people gathered. Left unsaid was Kinji's concern that the new launch might involve more unpleasant surprises. So far at least the weather had cooperated beyond their expectations, delivering up a mild seventy-degree average temperature and fair skies.

Serena was buoyed by the noise rising up from the people; it was like the buzzing of thousands of bees. She adjusted her green scarf, checked to make sure that her wrist band's power light was on, and surveyed the crowd. She was startled when she realized that all eyes were on her. She put her pilot's hat on. The crowd erupted.

On their feet, whistling, cheering, and even chanting something that Serena couldn't quite make out, it was clear that the people had chosen Serena Wilcox as their newest celebrity heroine—something that until now Serena had had no awareness of. She grinned and flashed them a big thumbs-up. Applause broke through the din.

Estep took her by the arm and growled, "Alright, don't let it go to your head. You have work to do."

"Don't worry, I always have you to keep me grounded." Serena allowed herself to be dragged toward Ruby Red until she caught Tom in her peripheral vision.

The new launch date had fit into his schedule, and since the event was now a big celebration, Tom and their three children were given box seats; which was really nothing more than GSI's best lobby furniture placed near the windows in the rotunda on the institute's highest level. They could opt to view the launch from the comfort of the rotunda's interior, or they could venture out onto the deck where the view was even better.

Serena had made sure that they had come prepared with cameras, snacks and even things to occupy themselves with in the event of long delays. She was confident that her family was all set. Barring a dead body in the portal, there wasn't anything to worry about.

Tom gave Serena a brief kiss and the crowd went wild. He waved at the portable stands, erected only two hours earlier, which were filled to their 10,000 person maximum capacity. When Carrie, Sam and Rebecca wrapped Serena in a group hug the crowd rallied again. Completely unfazed by the spotlight, Serena's family played to the crowd on their way to their VIP seating inside the institute.

Serena watched her husband and children as their backs disappeared into the lobby. It was a hollow feeling, watching her family leave without her. Suddenly her pilot hat felt heavy on her head and the scarf felt too tight around her neck.

Beav interrupted what he sensed were melancholy thoughts. "Hey, come on. You'll be back instantly, as if you've never been gone, remember? They won't even have time to miss you."

Serena fought back tears. "But I'll have time to miss them."

Estep responded, "Not if you never go! We're two minutes to launch."

Beav squeezed Serena's shoulder. "You'll be fine."

He and Estep stepped outside of the launch pad circle, joining the rest of the Project Scarecrow team. Of the fourteen original crew members Serena recognized Buick, Malirah, James Edison and honorary (consult) members Kendra, Jo, Lehman, and Beav. Roger, Eduardo, Gentry and Jorgi were gone, but that still left four crew members that she hadn't gotten to know beyond a simple introduction. She couldn't remember any of their names at the moment. This realization gave her pause. *Why didn't I dig a little deeper into the others?*

Serena was aware of cameras tracking her every move as she strode toward Ruby Red. She glanced up at the rotunda balcony. Tom and the kids waved. She blew kisses at them. The crowd shattered what had been a temporary lull in the peanut gallery. Cheers, whistles, and now even horns were added to the mix. Serena hastened her steps toward the time travel machine. She opened the door with her wristband—it was faster and easier than using the iris scanner. When the hatch opened the crowd roared.

Serena hesitated slightly, holding her breath. When no dead body materialized she hopped onto Ruby Red's seat. The media snapped hundreds of pictures of Serena on the chair in her traveling garb, smiling and waving seconds before the launch. As the crowd noise waned Serena took her cue to close the door of the time machine. She steadied herself and breathed a prayer for a safe trip. She paused a few seconds longer to say another prayer for her family. Then she opened the control panel and hit the green "go" button.

A fanfare went up when the crowd saw Ruby Red's flashing lights. In the next instant the entire shimmering metallic egg faded from view and the crowd roared. Serena Wilcox, first official time traveler, was gone. She was somewhere else in time and space, on a journey that the rest of them could only imagine. The crowd fell quiet in collective contemplation, a harmonious silence that they would share a memory of for the rest of their lives.

A mere two seconds later Ruby Red's lights were the first to re-appear, sweeping over the launch pad in spotlight fashion. The egg materialized immediately afterward: the time machine was back! A local high school band played "Space Explorers" by Kevin MacLeod. The crowd held their applause as everyone waited for the doors of the time machine to open.

The band played the song to the end of the arrangement but the hatch remained closed. Band members looked at each other, unsure whether or not they should play the song through a second time. It was when Beav and Estep ran toward the machine that everyone knew for sure that something must have gone wrong.

Tom was already on the ground, having nearly leapt down the three flights of stairs from the rotunda when the hatch didn't open. The three men drew closer to Ruby Red. Beav opened the door. The time machine was empty.

Natalie Buske Thomas

11

Serena's ears were ringing from the hideous pitch of the blood-curdling screams that had pelted Ruby Red's sound waves intermittently for the past two or three minutes. At first Serena had thought that the screams were her own---did something go horribly wrong with the time travel test run? Had she vaporized? Was she dead?

When she got her bearings she realized that the sound was definitely coming from outside of her body, and outside of Ruby Red itself, although not quite. It sounded as if the screams were coming from on top of Ruby Red, or maybe alongside of it. She heard a thud and then the screams stopped.

Serena sat in the time capsule for several minutes, listening. She heard nothing after the thud. She assumed that she had hit someone with her time machine, much like Dorothy had landed her house on the wicked witch. She hoped that she wouldn't find a dead body when she ventured out. Estep would never let her hear the end of it if she managed to leave yet another corpse in her wake, especially under these circumstances.

Thinking about Agent Estep reminded her of previous investigations that they had worked together. She then reflected back on her career overall, beginning with her first experience as a private detective. Serena's first case had been for herself.

She had left her purse in her car in her unlocked garage, which she admitted later to be a foolish thing to do, but her carelessness didn't negate the law. Stealing was stealing. Serena was incensed when she realized that her purse was missing.

This was back before paper checks became obsolete. Her bank had put a stop payment on the stolen checks, but Serena couldn't let it go. She followed the bank's records to all of the stores where the thieves had used her checks. Because her checks were customized with a Betty Boop design, store employees remembered them and were forthcoming with details about the thieves who forged her signature.

Serena gathered all of the clues and was hot on the trail of the stolen checkbook when she hit pay dirt: the last leg of the shopping spree included not one, but several local pizza deliveries. The thieves used their own home address, including a real name and phone number, to order over $75 worth of pizza delivered to their doorstep. Serena promptly added a side order of police officers to their doorstep.

The thieves matched the physical description given by employees from two other stores, where they had shopped for popular high-end basketball shoes before ordering pizza. While someone should have suspected that the ringleader of the group, a skinny white disheveled male with tattooed arms and a not-quite-sober expression, was probably not a fan of Betty Boop, it was the home pizza delivery that solved the case. Thus Serena Wilcox was known as the pizza detective, a moniker that she had long since dropped. Of course not all mysteries would be this easy to solve, but Serena was hooked.

She became a private investigator and worked mostly mundane and uneventful cases. She gained more visibility when she took on an in-vitro fertilization scam, a sabotaged virtual reality business, and a real estate con involving Internet message boards and a cult. She probably could have worked herself up to leasing a metro area building and taking on a few partners. However, her reputation would have been questionable, due to the oddball and unsavory cases that came her way.

She was spared a tawdry and crude future. When she married Tom she had relocated to follow his job. Later, her desire to stay home and raise children had derailed her career.

What she wouldn't give to go back to that simpler time—not when she was the pizza detective, but when she was in the middle of the good old days without even realizing it. Surveillance meant watching a butterfly kit for when a caterpillar would hatch from a cocoon, investigation meant tracking down the source of giggles by following a trail of tiny footprints, and hunting for a suspect meant finding the boy who had flown away in his blanket cape. Serena knew that it was against protocol to travel back in time to a point in her own life's history, but the temptation to travel back so that she could hold her babies once again was almost more than she could resist.

Here she was, somewhere in time and space, alone. And in that void she was acutely aware of what was most important to her, who she loved, and what she had lost. She regretted that her children didn't have ties to a childhood home, something that she herself had missed out on and had wanted to change for the next generation.

Serena had no real roots. She had moved around too many times, both as a child and then later as an adult. Even when she stayed in one location for over fifteen years, certainly long enough for most people to feel native, the mishmash of local accents she had picked up over the course of her lifetime gave her away as a transplant and an outsider. While she had had many friends, friends always disappeared when holidays approached; holidays are for family.

Invites to other families' private parties were always awkward—she had learned to turn those invitations down. No, Serena wasn't attached to any one area. Her home was wherever she was living with her husband and her kids at the time. And she thought that she was fine with that. But now, sitting in another dimension, alone, everything was in sharp focus.

Serena promised herself that when she was done traveling through time and space she would go home. And by "home" she meant that she wanted to live in a place where she belonged, a place where she and Tom could grow old together and rock their grandbabies on their front porch. She knew that she hadn't yet found that place.

Probably the biggest reason why Serena hadn't made a home connection was because her great grandparents, grandparents and parents were all deceased. She regretted that she hadn't yet found her Irish ancestors. Maybe then she would feel that she had roots. She wondered if Jo might be willing to help her with that. Serena reflected that she could live anywhere she wanted to—*why not Ireland?*

But why stop there? She could live anywhere in *time* that she wanted to live, assuming that such a thing wouldn't cause a paradox. She could live in the past, before the tragedies of her generation, and the generations before hers, changed what it means to be safe and free. She'd be wealthy if she brought currency with her. She imagined herself without a care in the world, growing fruit trees. *Why fruit trees?* Her thoughts drifted over the possibilities of time, space, accidentally meeting her former self and many other tangled musings, the last of which involved seeing her grandfather and running to stay one step ahead of him seeing her.

The next thing Serena was cognizant of was waking up, wiping drool off of her cheek with the back of her hand, and orienting herself to where she was. She opened the control panel, read the digital display and said aloud, "I've been asleep for twenty minutes!"

Her words hung in Ruby Red's tiny airspace. She realized that she never thought to ask how much air she had in there. She was dizzy and had a headache.

139

Is there some kind of ventilation system? Maybe that's why I fell asleep. Is my brain deprived of oxygen? She slid off the chair, teetered on the doorway ledge and scrabbled at the door until the hatch opened. She stumbled out of the portal and took in large gulps of air.

She looked around. There was nothing much to see. *What is it with me and cornfields?* A cornfield had been a big part of her Covert Coffee adventure. She hoped that corn wouldn't be a reoccurring theme in her new career as a time traveling detective.

She closed the hatch using her wristband. She kept one finger hovering over the hatch button, just in case she needed to dart back inside the capsule. Then she maneuvered around Ruby Red, examining the ground and the exterior of the portal for the source of the thud that she'd heard when she materialized onto the field, or "landed". Even though she knew that the concept of flight had nothing to with the physics of time travel it was hard not to think in those terms.

She found a dark substance on the side of the metallic egg. She couldn't tell if the substance was blood, since Ruby Red's coloring and finish made it difficult to tell, but she was fairly sure that it was indeed human blood. She didn't want to touch it to find out. She gave it a sniff test. Yes, it smelled like copper. She followed the blood trail with her eyes. It looked like someone had been splatted onto Ruby Red.

Serena wondered how that could have happened. Why would someone have been suspended above the ground in the exact time and place for a collision to have been possible? Her next question was: where did the mysterious struck-by-a-time-machine victim go?

Serena didn't have to wait long for an answer. She heard voices coming from a tree row that separated the cornfield from an adjacent field that had soy beans in it. She squatted low to the ground like a duck and waddled her way toward the corn. She crept as close as she dared and hunkered down between the rows.

"It about killed me! I thought my skin had torn off my hide," said the taller of the two.

"But it didn't and you're able to walk now. We've already burned up about half an hour."

"You didn't say it was going to hurt like hell. I could have died, you don't know."

"Get over it. We're on a time line. If she gets to it first we're done here. We get it, we get out."

"Why would she know anything about this?"

"She shouldn't. But she's here. She'll see us eventually if we stand around like jackals."

Serena would have loved to have ended her game of hide and seek with a big "Peek-a-boo, I see you!" but what then? Whatever was going on, she knew she had to ask for backup.

She made her way back to Ruby Red, which wasn't hard, given that she hadn't wandered far from it. She opened the hatch, hopped onto the seat, and searched for the keypad she remembered seeing. She found it, typed a message, and sent Ruby Red back to the launching pad without her in it.

12

"A hush fell over the crowd" was an appropriate cliché to describe what happened when the hatch opened and Ruby Red was obviously empty. Tom, Lehman, Beav and Estep were now all four scrambling to examine the time machine, as if by doing so Serena would suddenly appear. Since only one of them could fit in there at a time there was a mad jockeying for position until Beav reminded them that he knew the interior of Ruby Red better than anyone. He went inside, popped the control panel open, and brought up the screen display.

"She's okay!" He backed out of the hatch, whirled around and yelled in the direction of the stands, "She made it! Serena Wilcox has landed!"

The media was all over Beav, shoving multiple microphones in his face. He waved Lehman over and rasped in his ear, "I have a thing about hearing my own voice."

Lehman was an old pro by now, having delivered dozens of press conferences during his brief stint as the emergency appointee Vice President near the end of Kinji's administration. He knew how to appear as if he was giving information without really saying much of anything. Best of all, he had great showmanship and stage presence.

Tom used this distraction to zip into the machine to read Serena's message: "I'm OK, but you need to postpone my return so that you can clear everyone out – should be returning with two men in custody, don't think Ann would want that kind of PR. They arrived at the same time I did (from here, from our time). Can you make a lot of trips in the time machine? I could use a whole team here. Tell Tom and the kids that I'm fine and I love them. PS: Bring money or food."

Tom climbed back out of the machine. He addressed Estep and Beav. "I want to go."

Estep shook his head. "No can do. We'll get her back. We've been down this road before."

"Not like this." Tom stared at Ruby Red.

Estep went through the hatch to read Serena's message while Beav reassured

Tom. "You of all people know that we don't need this machine. I came to you for advice on the design. We've been putting on a show for Serena's sake, and for publicity and patriotism too if I think about it. We don't need it though, remember? We can easily send an entire extraction team to her, and we will."

Beav stopped talking to tune in to Lehman's impromptu press conference. In his opening statement Lehman sold everyone on the idea that Serena had already started her first mission. He was able to spin a yarn that was both plausible and noble, leaving the crowd pumped and expectant. Worldwide, people would be watching the news tomorrow for an update, an update that would be mostly fiction. Lehman promised pictures of Serena's triumphant return. Victory and adventure had been sold to the media and to the spectators with no problems whatsoever.

Victory wasn't an easy sell to Ann Kinji or to the crew, however. Their anxiety was palpable. Ann had made an abrupt change of plans from her public relations agenda. She turned up at Beav's side while he was resuming his conversation with Tom about the extraction team.

Beav explained, "I'll give them wristbands. We made an entire assembly line of them when we were testing them out. I think we have..." He stopped talking in mid-sentence, then turned around and ran toward GSI. Estep was close at his heels.

Everyone else ambled over at a less dramatic pace---there were still media personalities lingering in the vicinity; it was better that they didn't all run like a pack of wild boars and tip the media off to the unfolding drama. Before they even reached the doors Ann pulled Tom aside. "Beav's in my ear. Looks like we already have a break in the case. Apparently someone stole a couple wristbands, he ran in to verify his hunch. Now that we know how the two men got there, we can re-program the bands." Ann patted him on the arm. "We've got this, Tom. Please take the kids and go home. Serena is in good hands."

The kids were still on the balcony, unsure of what to do. Tom took one look at their troubled faces and knew that Ann was right; he needed to get them home. He had to trust that everything would turn out fine. He comforted himself with the fact that Serena sounded confident in the tone of her message.

Tom wasn't the only one who was asked to leave. Ruby Red's namesake, Ruby the secretary, shooed the press out of the lobby. She also ushered everyone else out the door who was loitering. Even people twice her size and half her age did what she asked without question. After the building was cleared of everyone who didn't work for GSI Ruby released non-essential crew members, including herself. The only people who remained were core team members and Agent Estep's newly assembled extraction team.

By this time Beav had counted and re-counted the inventory of wristbands. Exactly two bands were missing. Beav briefed Ann and the crew. "Gentry was the last person logged into the room where the wristbands were stored. Gentry was found dead in the time machine on launch day. A + B = C. I assume that Jorgi was lurking about and slipped in when Gentry was entering the room. He took the bands and killed Gentry before he could report the theft."

Estep scoffed. "Easy to blame the dead guy."

Beav said, "Good point. Where's Eduardo?"

"That's enough speculating." Ann turned toward Agent Estep. "Go get Serena."

Estep sought clarification. "Are we to bring the two men back? Or can we zap them back like you told Tom?"

"Bring them in after Serena is out of the way. Your priority is Serena Wilcox. And no, we can't 'zap them back'. Reprogramming takes time. Treat this like you would any other arrest--- find them, cuff them, and bring them in."

Beav cleared his throat. "I hate to bring this up, because I know we have enough to worry about."

Ann gave him her full attention.

Beav spoke while distributing wristbands to Estep's extraction team.

"The longer they stay in there, the greater the odds are that they have messed with the natural order of things. For every tree branch they disturb, they may cause someone to trip who was never meant to fall. For every resource they consume, they may take away from someone else who was meant to have it. For every..."

"Got it." Ann turned toward Estep. "I'm counting on you to do what you do best."

Estep's face beamed. "Yes, Ma'am."

His face fell when Ann clarified what she meant. "Fetch Serena."

Estep's team sniggered and chortled as they followed their stormy leader out of GSI. Ann waited until the extraction team was out of earshot before asking Beav, "How serious is this business about messing with the natural order of things?"

"It's a matter of physics."

Ann frowned. "Meaning?"

153

Beav shrugged. "How serious is the law of gravity when a piano is dropped from a plane?"

Ann quipped, "I don't know, are we standing under it?"

"We're smack in the middle of the drop zone."

"Then why are you still here?" Ann stared meaningfully at Beav until he left.

13

Mandolin shed his hospital custodian uniform and threw it into the nearest Dumpster. Then he backtracked and retrieved it from the Dumpster. He had seen enough television to know that the uniform would be found by some kid and reported to the police. He was better off if he buried it. For now he stuffed the uniform into his bag.

The sound of tires crunching over gravel caught his attention. He recognized the black Lexus as the same one that had followed Jorgi. Obviously this power player wasn't loyal to his people, what with Jorgi dead and all. But then again, Mandolin hadn't been loyal either, what with killing Jorgi and all. Mandolin got in the car.

The driver didn't take long to get to the point. "Is it done?"

Mandolin studied the man's face, but it was hard to get a read on him under the brim of his hat, behind his shades, and around the poorly applied synthetic facial hair. Mandolin relaxed. Because the man was disguising his identity, Mandolin was reasonably certain that he wasn't planning to kill him. He answered with confidence. "It's done. But I'm curious, why come to me? I told your man Jorgi everything I got out of Roger. You have Eduardo—why kill Jorgi?"

"He had become a liability."

"From what I saw he was a professional." Mandolin knew that he must be missing something.

"He didn't tell me what Roger told you. I had to find you myself, which wasn't easy."

"Ah, he got greedy. He held back for more money?" Mandolin had experienced similar situations with his own employees. It was hard to get good help these days.

"No."

"You've lost me. Why didn't he deliver on the job?" Mandolin pressed the issue, knowing that at some point his inquiry would be shut down. He was taken aback when his question was answered.

"He was a double agent."

The hair on Mandolin's neck stood up. Gangsters, mobsters, ex-cons, thugs and even psychos were his world. But spooks? He had nothing to do with the underbelly of government agencies and their fancy technology, their Ivy League spies and old money calling the shots. Jobs for hire he understood; he killed relatively bad people for cash--- but he was no monster. He popped the door open, even though the Lexus was still in motion. He estimated that the vehicle was going under thirty miles per hour; he figured he could tuck and roll, even though a big guy like himself wouldn't come away from such a stunt without some serious damage.

The driver anticipated Mandolin's move and flat-footed the accelerator. Mandolin struggled to close the door. "All right, you got me. I'm staying."

"Mandolin, I'm not going to hurt you. I have no reason to. You don't have any connection to foreign operatives, or domestic for that matter."

Mandolin grunted.

"All right then, there's no reason to bail. I promised cash payment and you'll find it in the bag under your seat. I appreciate your service to your country."

Mandolin's broad face softened. He had always wanted to be a Marine but he couldn't stay out of trouble. "I'm listening."

"We had the wristbands, but we didn't know how to program them. Roger made it clear that we needed Eduardo. You delivered. Because of you, time travel is possible."

"Hold up, how am I helping my country? If you were on our side you wouldn't need me."

The driver stopped the car. He ripped off his facial hair, exposing his cheekbones and chin, revealing a Caucasian face that was ordinarily well groomed but today exposed reddish stubble. His voice took on a cool even tone; controlled, devoid of emotion, and in Mandolin's mind downright chilling. "You've seen part of my face. You know what I'll have to do to you if you see the rest of it."

Mandolin grabbed the false beard and tossed it into the backseat. He refused to let him rattle his cage. "So you're saying that you aren't one of the good guys? You aren't working for my government?"

"Those are two different questions."

Mandolin's blood pressure rose. "I'm a cowboy in a black hat. There's a big difference between an outlaw and a terrorist. I'm no piss-ant coward traitor."

The driver laughed. "I like you, Mandolin. Get out of the car."

Mandolin got out. The driver immediately pulled a gun on him, but it was too late. One of Mandolin's men fired first. Too far away to do any real damage, the shot—with seven more to follow--

served only as cover for Mandolin to escape in a classic Lamborghini Diablo. The man in the Lexus took off in the opposite direction, but not before Mandolin had given him a going away present.

Unbeknownst to the driver, not all of those fired rounds were bullets. One of the shots contained a tracking device that had been fired from an ordinary gun, holding up to the hype that sold Mandolin on the device. The device, when successfully aimed, was designed to hold fast to any hard surface target-- especially an automobile exterior, which was what the tracker was intended for. Mandolin's guy had scored a direct hit. The tracker was already live and following the Lexus' every move.

Mandolin chuckled. "Spooks don't have all the techie toys. This cowboy's been upgraded."

161

His gunman said, "I don't understand half of what you say, Boss."

Mandolin kept an eye on the rearview mirror. He found the vanishing tail lights of the Lexus gratifying. When he was satisfied that the spook was not coming back he placed a call to the only man he knew who could handle himself in the underbelly of government spies and demons.

14

Serena was hunkered down in a cornfield. The stench of corn maze failure and hide-and-seek terror from her childhood assaulted her senses. Added to these experiences was the infamous corn field adventure during Operation Covert Coffee. The musk and the mildew, the insects and the worms, the smell of the corn and the grit; it all came back to her. These memories became tiresome as boredom set in.

It wasn't long before the tedium of the wait was replaced by unbearable itching as the mosquitos lit into her. Serena pressed an X pattern into her bites with her fingernails to give herself relief from the welts. She made a mental note to carry bug repellent with her in the future, or in the past, whichever was more accurate to say. Finally, as the sun set on the tasseled horizon and there was still no sign of Ruby Red, she emerged from the corn.

"There she is!" One of Estep's evacuation team announced her presence.

"Have you been hiding in there the whole time?" Estep asked; his tone more of condemnation than concern.

Beav said, "That would be a good thing. You were right here? Touching nothing, doing nothing?"

Serena looked from one to the other. "I followed the two men. I didn't touch anything."

"What? Oh no. Did you talk to anyone? Well of course you did. Where did you go? What did you do exactly?" Beav tried to guess how many hours Serena had been roaming around, inadvertently altering history wherever she went. He whipped off his bandana and jammed it into his denim back pocket. After his hair fell damp and lifeless onto his hot skin he put the bandana back on.

"Did you choose this location?" Serena asked.

Beav answered slowly, not understanding why she was asking. "No, that wasn't me. Eduardo programmed the bands weeks ago."

Estep interjected, "Is this important to figure out right now? We're standing around in the dark doing nothing."

Serena ignored Estep and continued her conversation with Beav. "I didn't realize that you had more wristbands besides my own until I saw the two men wearing one. I suppose that's how all of you got here. How many of those things do you have?" She strained her eyes to see across the field. "Did anyone even use Ruby Red? I don't see it."

Beav said, "The time machine is all yours, I wouldn't think of driving your car."

"I see. It would have been nice if you'd told me that you had an entire inventory of them." Serena tried not to take it personally.

"We were prepared in case we needed to go looking for you." Beav smoothed things over as quickly as he could. "Not that we don't trust you."

Estep grumbled. "I don't trust her. Let's go find out what she did."

Beav shook his head, though no one could see him now that it was getting dark. "That's the thing, we can't. Can you imagine if people saw an extraction team from the future strolling down the street?"

Estep said, "When and where are we anyway?"

Beav scolded, "You seriously never read any of my memos do you?"

Estep was quick to point out that Beav sent him so many messages that he'd have to quit his day job to read them all, which was yet another way to slip in a reminder that he was still employed as a federal agent, lest anyone forget it.

"We'll wait for them to come back to this spot---it's the only way that they can travel," said Beav. "They haven't had time to reprogram the bands either. I can't emphasize enough that if we don't catch these guys there will be disastrous consequences. Whoever they are working for has access to Eduardo and after he reprograms the bands they'll be completely on the loose wherever and whenever they want to go, all over time and space."

Serena agreed. "I'll add this cheery thought: I asked you who chose the location because if it wasn't you, and you confirmed that it wasn't, isn't it possible that when Eduardo programmed the bands he had an agenda? I assumed his test launch pick was random. I mean, who goes to Iowa? With the infinite choices available, why would *anyone* choose to go to Iowa? I thought he was selecting a remote rural area so that no one would see me and Ruby Red pop in and out."

Beav's voice cracked. "I thought Eduardo was a victim. If he's behind this it could be too late to stop them."

Serena spoke quickly to avoid being interrupted by Agent Estep. "He may be a victim, acting under coercion. After all, someone killed Gentry---they could have threatened Eduardo. Regardless of

168

Eduardo's motives, he had to have been helping them all along; this location was intentional. Without a doubt the two men knew exactly where they were going. They had a GPS that led them directly to the Blackhawk Hotel, the Pompeian Room to be precise. I followed them from a safe distance, but then I had no choice but to bail. I didn't have any money. How could I get away with dawdling outside a luxury restaurant without someone noticing me?"

"You came right back here?" Beav felt some of the tension in his shoulders ease up.

"Yes, I came back here. By the way, those two didn't cause any problems from what I could see. They wore the right clothes and blended in. Speaking of blending in, I left my pilot's hat and scarf back here, stashed between the corn rows. I wore period piece clothes under my contemporary wardrobe. I came prepared--

-you need to give me more credit. Rest assured, no one gave me more than a passing glance. I didn't see my grandfather."

Beav was the only one who laughed at Serena's cerebral joke reference to seeing her grandfather. She scowled. "I do have a bone to pick with you, Beav. When you ran down your list of complications that could arise if I was ever trapped inside Ruby Red, you mentioned that I had movies to entertain myself. You mentioned enough food and water to last me for days. You were awfully concerned about my need to pee. But hadn't you left something out?" When Beav didn't reply right away she continued, "Isn't there *anything* else you can think of that I might need to stay alive? Food, water, shelter… Air! Oxygen, Beav. I nearly passed out."

Beav's jaw dropped, but again it was hard to see his expression in the darkness.

"I have to admit that there may be an oversight in this area."

Estep thought to ask, "Why were you trapped?"

"Those men arrived when I did and there was a nasty collision. I stayed inside until I thought it was safe to come out."

Estep's extraction team had grown restless and requested an update. Serena wasn't the only one getting eaten alive by mosquitos. Estep instructed his team to disperse into the corn and soy bean fields. "Prepare to take a shot if you have to. We need to take these two in, one way or another. Superficial injuries only—we need them awake and ready for interrogation."

Estep's team barely had time to get into position before the two men returned. One of them said, "She's already left. The egg is gone." They stretched their arms out in unison in readiness to use the bands.

The coordinated movement amused Serena, who couldn't resist smarting off.

She called out, "Before you Wonder Twins activate, you should know that you are surrounded by federal agents."

The two men reached for their bands but the agents were faster than they were. Each man was shot in the ankles by no fewer than seven rounds. They crumpled to the ground with a thud not unlike the sound that Serena had heard from inside Ruby Red.

Estep yelled at his extraction team. "This isn't an arcade! *You* shot them, *you're* carrying them!" He continued to grumble. "This is the best team GSI could give me?"

Serena finished his thoughts, "Which is why you can never quit your day job."

Estep snorted. "Leave my day job alone. *You* are why I can never quit *this* job."

Upon their return to the Gödel Solution Institute, and back to the present day, the two men were immediately shuttled off to an interrogation room. Agent Estep made it abundantly and redundantly clear that he had fired the B-Team and was now assembling a team from his own list. No one objected or even seemed to care how Estep ran the investigation. Everyone had their own jobs to do.

The core team met briefly to compare notes. Lehman had found nothing of consequence in GSI's records. The surveillance system had been shut down when the bands were stolen. It was already assumed that Jorgi was the inside man and Lehman found nothing to either confirm or deny that assumption: they were prepared to accept it at face value. The investigation was focused on finding Eduardo. They were optimistic that Agent

173

Estep would get that information out of the men that they had in custody.

Meanwhile, Serena called upon Nicholas and Marco, two teenage geniuses she had worked with before. Between the two of them the boys loaded her control panel with more data on Davenport, Iowa than she could realistically read. She made a hurried attempt to educate herself on Davenport, the Blackhawk Hotel, and 1939.

Although time travel theoretically allowed her to stop time, the events of the present day were clipping along at a fast pace. It would be complicated, and full of potential paradoxes, to orchestrate an investigation in such a way that they had the luxury of time. It was best to do this old school: solve the case by working fast. So she skimmed the Iowa research and as soon as she thought that she had a fuzzy idea of what 1939 was all about, she

174

pressed the green go button to return to Davenport.

Natalie Buske Thomas

15

The first thing Serena did when Ruby Red landed in the now-familiar cornfield was check her appearance in the mirrored control panel cover. She smiled, thinking how irritated Roger McCloy would be if he knew that she was using the control panel as a makeup mirror after all. She smoothed her floral button-down dress unnecessarily; the fabric hadn't wrinkled on the instantaneous journey back to Davenport,

Iowa 1939. However, she did have to be mindful of the possibility of catching her shoe on the hem of her dress as she hopped down from Ruby Red's unusually high chair.

Today's launch had been without any fanfare—it had been just Beav sending her off with a two-fingered salute. Her assignment this time was simple, but it was an official undercover mission nonetheless. Her objectives were to arrive the day before her test launch date, retrace her steps to the Pompeian Room in the Blackhawk Hotel, and attach a listening device under the table where she knew the two men would be seated the next day. Apparently the mission was too small for anyone to bother to assign an operation name to it. Serena dubbed it Operation Blackhawk, team of one.

The walk to the Blackhawk Hotel was relaxed. She had selected penny loafers instead of heels and she found them so comfortable that she considered adopting them into her contemporary wardrobe. She had money with her this time, although it had cost GSI much more than face value and provoked an irked head-wag of Ann Kinji's famous bob.

Jo and Malirah had purchased most of the money from coin collectors to make sure that none of the coins were minted after 1939. The good news was that a dollar stretched far and almost made up for the cost of buying money from coin collectors. Serena could eat anything that she wanted from the Pompeian Room without looking at the prices.

Being extravagant was a foreign concept to her though, and she couldn't quite bring herself to the point of not thinking of the cost at all. Serena recalled bringing her lunch to school, when a sandwich was a single slice of processed cheese on Wonder Bread. A vacation was a long drive in the family's small car to visit relatives. There was no extra money for things like piano lessons, orthodontics, or a college education, but they had never gone homeless—they were far from that at least.

Although Serena had bettered her financial situation from those childhood days, not every month was a good one. Her paycheck from GSI wasn't nearly as much as people assumed that it was, and her new celebrity status was worthless. On a positive note, her finances were private. Even Ann Kinji didn't know how meager Serena's salary was, as the paychecks were cut at the federal level and weren't seen by the CEO or anyone else outside of accounting. However, if Ann had been made aware of how little her team was paid, surely she would have done something about it. In this way, the hybrid nature of GSI was failing Serena Wilcox.

Serena's husband Tom was also struggling to earn a fair paycheck after the company he worked for had given him yet another pay cut. All while the family's living expenses had gone up. The five of them had been living off of peanut butter sandwiches, tuna fish, and crackers—a situation that Serena had kept to herself. It was all temporary, she reminded herself. *This is just a rough patch.*

But sitting here in the Pompeian Room she felt as if everyone could see right into her soul. They could see the trailer that was her first childhood home, and they could see that, more than forty years later, her bank account proved that she was no better off than the day that she was born. She now had a mortgage that made it all *seem* better, but who was she kidding? She half expected someone to tell her that she wasn't dressed well enough.

181

No matter how fancy her clothes, she knew her place, and it wasn't at this table.

Serena Wilcox was ditzy, adventurous, impish and gutsy, but seldom vulnerable. It occurred to her that she was not enjoying her meal as much as she thought that she would. As she felt like the room was closing in on her she wished that she was seated near a window. She picked up a cloth napkin and laid it in her lap. She remembered at least that much about how to eat at a formal table. Unfortunately she had no idea which fork to use and she was equally perplexed about what to do with her fork after she used it. The idea of eating an entire dinner with this much attention to etiquette was exhausting.

Her mood brightened considerably when she remembered that she was here on a spy mission. She was a time traveler, the first official time traveler the world had ever known. *Is it really important that I don't know which fork to use?* Serena savored every last bite of her meal when she rebelliously ate the rest of it entirely with her soup spoon.

Natalie Buske Thomas

16

Mandolin spoke quickly.

"Eduardo?"

"Yes."

"Everyone's listening."

"Yes."

"I can get a message to GSI."

Eduardo responded in a strained voice, "Please don't call this frequency again. I'll be six feet under and so will you. For whom the bell tolls, eight, nine, and twelve."

The line went dead.

Mandolin slipped his phone into a plastic bag. He rolled up to the GSI gate, a few yards from where he was idling. He threw the bag over the gate and waited until he was a safe distance away before calling the Gödel Solution Institute to let them know that the phone was there.

Lehman analyzed the phone's data and zeroed in immediately on the call placed to Eduardo. He replayed it in Kinji's office.

Beav said, "He mentioned a frequency of 668912. That's not more than fifteen miles from here."

Ann was astounded. "How did you come up with that?"

Beav emphasized the number words while repeating what Eduardo had said. "I'll be 6 feet under and so will you' (add a second 6). The last four digits followed his 'for whom the bell tolls' quote. As for 'frequency', that's the term we use when programming a time travel location. Eduardo told us where he is when he said frequency 668912. I'll wager it's a building and suite number for the complex on Hemingway Avenue."

Ann was flabbergasted. "Insider language aside, that's still incredibly fast to come up with that, especially the street and building number! I only got as far as 'for whom the bell tolls', Hemingway."

Beav laughed. "I have to confess. Lehman pinged the phone. I solved the riddle after already knowing the solution."

"Ah, I see. Well, what are you waiting for? Did you tell Estep?" Ann asked.

"Already done." Lehman assured her. "Estep should be there now." He pulled up the surveillance footage from the gala. "We scanned the phone for prints. Mandolin Fredrik is in the system, so my hunch is that you'll recognize him."

187

Ann peered at the screen. "His mug shot isn't very impressive."

"I know, that new system they have is absurd. If they're going to do an upgrade they should at least train their people how to…" Lehman felt Kinji's impatience. He moved on. "I had trouble getting an exact match to the video feed from the party. But if he was at the gala, your memory of seeing him in person could help." Lehman used a split screen to show both the mug shot and the video footage at the same time.

Ann pointed to Mandolin in the gala footage. "Oh yes, this is him, he's the same man from the mug shot. I recognize the nose---it's been broken a few times."

Beav said, "I asked Estep to round up all of the ex-cons from the gala, but I must warn you, I'm not jazzed."

Ann tilted her head. "Why?"

188

Beav fiddled with the knot on his bandana. "He said that his team is stretched thin. They're on site to retrieve Eduardo. So, he sent the B-Team to round up Mandolin and his mates. It was either that, or we had to wait for Estep's team to be free."

Ann shook her head. "Oh we can't wait." But waiting is what they did do. They alternated between making small talk and resting quietly in the calm before the storm.

About an hour later Lehman switched to the live-feed view of GSI's front security gate. "The B-Team's here now."

Beav pointed at the screen. "There's Estep right behind them. They're all here at the same time."

Ann sighed. "This is the kind of madness I thought I'd left behind."

Beav's face fell.

Ann noticed. "What now?"

Beav scowled at his phone's text messages. "Serena wants me to reprogram her wristband to a new frequency and she wants intelligence." His phone buzzed again. "And she wants assistance too! She's sitting on the launch pad right now. I can't be two places at once."

"We're talking about time travel. Can't you be two places at once?" Ann chuckled. When Beav didn't crack a smile she added, "I'm throwing a bit of brevity your way. I know what it takes to do these launches."

"Send Jo. She's been training to be a field operative," Lehman suggested.

Beav said, "She has? This is the first I've heard of it."

Ann clarified. "She's a citizen of the Republic of Ireland. Everything she does for us is unofficial."

Beav tipped his imaginary hat. "Welcome to my world. Everything I do is unofficial." His brow furrowed when he realized that he had added another programming errand to his list. "I'll get her set up with a wristband."

Lehman suggested, "As for research, put Nicholas and Marco on it, they've already proven that they can do it. They're younger and faster than I am at putting things like that together."

Ann smiled. "Are you feeling old, Lehman?"

"Old and homesick," he said.

"Point taken." Ann reassured him, "I don't anticipate keeping you on for much longer. It seems that everything here is wrapping up nicely."

Beav rapped on Ann's desk.

Lehman and Ann both looked at him, startled.

He said, "I'm knocking on wood."

"You should have knocked louder," said Lehman, when they saw the mob waiting for them in the lobby.

191

Ruby materialized as if by magic, reminding everyone of her time machine namesake. Her Hawaiian style blouse and her large jangly gold earrings brought festivity into a room full of people clad in a near colorless assortment of casual earth tones, gray athletic wear, and black suits. But festivity didn't overtake Ruby's imposing presence, which was surpassed only by Ann's immediate leadership.

"Ruby, sort this chaos into four groups. Estep, Beav, Lehman and I will each take a room. When you're finished with that, send for Jo. Actually, we could use everybody. Bring them all in; everyone we still have left anyway."

Estep hurried to Ann's ear. "With all due respect President Kinji, should you be interrogating suspects yourself?"

Ann pooh-poohed his lecture. "It's private citizen Kinji now, and this is my company. I have a way of getting people to talk to me. It might surprise you."

Estep replied, "Nothing you do would surprise me, but I have to take issue with your use of the phrase 'private citizen'. I don't think you've cut those governmental apron strings as much as you think you have."

"Your objection is duly noted." Ann then clapped her hands and said, "Let's get these tongues wagging!"

17

Serena was startled to see Jo walking toward Ruby Red's launch pad. "Has Beav sent you to assist me?"

"If you'll have me. It's either this or I have to interrogate suspects. I choose this."

"I'm delighted!" Serena glanced at the time machine, wondering if the two of them could fit inside it. There seemed to be enough room if one of them stood behind the seat.

"He said all I need is the band." Jo held up her wrist.

"Yes, I know, but it's not the same as traveling by time machine. We can both fit. One of us can stand in the back."

"You sit, I'll stand. I'm taller than you. The platform behind the chair looks made for me."

Serena said proudly, "You're right! You were destined to be my co-pilot. Girl Power!" She extended her arm for a fist bump.

Jo laughed. "Sure." She tapped Serena's fist. Then she stepped into the portal and positioned herself on the platform behind the seat. She had just enough space for her feet to fit comfortably.

Serena leapt onto the seat and closed the hatch. "I didn't brief you on what we're doing."

"Can't you do that on the way?"

"Oh no, once I hit 'go' we'll be there instantly."

"I'm not strapped in—this doesn't bounce around?" Jo's voice was a bit shaky.

"Not at all. There'll be a satisfying *whoosh* sound and the lights will flicker, and it will get dark, as if you've blinked your eyes. And that's it—we'll fade out of one dimension and fade into another. I suspect that Beav added the whoosh sound effect for drama. I won't tell him that I'm on to him."

"He won't hear it from me." Jo gave her a slow wink. It was difficult not to give in to giggles, since she knew full well that the *entire concept* of the time machine had been manufactured just for Serena. Then it dawned on her: Serena was the most respected, most renowned female sleuth she had ever met; regardless of the silly persona she was so fond of projecting. What are the odds that Serena was hoodwinked by this whole affair? *Zero*, Jo decided. "Serena, what do you know about time travel technology?"

Serena's face was suddenly dark as she turned around in her seat to stare at Jo. "I was the child who hated magic shows. I found them tedious and boring. Why? Because I knew that everything was a trick, and most of the time I could figure out how the act was done. But I've always believed in Santa Claus without question. Jo, it took a lot of hours for Santa's elves to make Ruby Red for me."

"Understood. I won't say a word. Although I must say, I have a hard time telling the difference between when you're serious and when you aren't."

"That makes two of us." Serena held her hand over the green 'go' button. "Are you ready?"

Jo pumped her fist in the air. "Let 'er whoosh!"

Serena pressed the green button. She kept her eyes open so that she wouldn't miss the nearly-instantaneous fading sensation of going from the present into the past. The *whoosh* didn't disappoint. She waited for the lights to stop flashing before she opened the hatch, exited the time machine, and said, "Not a bad ride, wouldn't you say?"

"As long as my molecules all arrived in the same position and the same place I'll agree with you."

Within the half hour Jo and Serena strolled side-by-side down the residential streets of Davenport, Iowa 1939, their inequity in height a comical sight. Serena had browsed through a couple more file

199

folders about the history of Davenport before Jo had arrived on the landing pad. She filled Jo in on some of the background on the area.

"In 1931 The RKO Orpheum Theatre-Mississippi Hotel complex opened; boasting Iowa's largest movie house. It was the year that *The Wizard of Oz* and *Gone with the Wind* had premiered." Try as she might, Serena couldn't find any information about whether or not the Orpheum had premiered either of the two biggest movies ever made—history could be in the making at that very moment in Davenport, Iowa, or not. She hoped to take a peek at the marquee on the theater building itself, since it wasn't but a short walk from the Blackhawk Hotel. Of course she was getting distracted, she chided herself. They didn't have time to go to the movies, no matter how tempting it was to see the premiere of a classic film!

Not a moment later, she couldn't help but be captivated by a large farmhouse style home at the end of the block. There were about a dozen people of all ages and sizes gathered on, off, and on top of the spacious porch. The scene looked like a movie set. It almost made up for missing out on going to the cinema.

There was an elderly man sitting on a rocking chair, a young boy wearing what looked like new church shoes, sitting on the railing, and several more people seated on wooden kitchen chairs. Two of the men who were standing rested one foot on a step or a railing, while the bulk of their weight rested on their standing leg. The stance seemed vaguely familiar, as if they might be imitating the posture of movie stars that were popular at the time, like Clark Cable or Cary Grant.

A little girl wore white Mary Janes and a matching white bow in hair that was

201

bobbed and curled into thick coils. Her dress was short, several inches above the knee, while the women wore long dresses that fell several inches below the knee. All of the women, including the girls, wore floral print dresses of a similar style; short-sleeved, with a blouse-like bodice, and tied in the back. The women wore hats, which was a fashion statement that Serena wished was still in vogue.

The men also wore hats. Those who didn't wear hats parted their hair on the side and slicked it back away from their foreheads with what looked like the same brand of hair oil. Serena imagined that they might have shared the tin and passed it around. All of the men, including the boys, wore collared shirts. Some wore ties as well, and one of the men was even wearing a full suit. All of them wore dressy shoes that gleamed. Shoe-shining hadn't yet fallen out of favor.

"Hey, Old Salts, there're two for you!" they heard one of them say.

The man presumed to be "Old Salts" tipped his hat in their direction. He was dashingly handsome and he knew it. He set his sights on Jo.

"Smile, wave, walk on," Serena said under her breath.

When they had cleared hearing range of the porch Jo said, "Old Salts is fresh out of the Navy I assume?"

"Probably. We can't interact with people here. We'd better press on."

Jo reminded her, "You haven't told me where we're going."

"I put a bug under the table where our mystery men were eating. They mentioned going to The Iowa Soldiers' Orphans' Home, which isn't far away. We'll be up on it soon."

"When? Have they already been there? And why?"

"One of them went there while the other stayed in the restaurant. Yes. Long story."

Jo laughed. "Getting three separate answers from you at the same time is confusing. I'll ask only one question at a time in the future."

"Or in the past."

"Right. What a strange feeling this is." Jo observed that even the trees looked younger.

"It looks like we've walked into a classic car show, doesn't it?" Serena admired the vintage cars adorning the streets, although of course these vehicles wouldn't be considered classics for decades yet. The Duesenberg, also known by its nickname the "Duesy", caught her attention, but she had no clue about the name of this car, or the year that it was made (1935), and likely the only reason why she noticed the car at all was because it was shiny and red. When she tried to describe the Duesenberg later to the crew, her description was too vague for anyone to know what she was talking about. All she remembered was that the car was a convertible, it had a tan top, and there was a spare white tire on the body of the car itself. Besides vehicles, there were plenty of pedestrians out and about today as well. Serena knew much more about people than she did cars.

They passed two little girls on the sidewalk, obviously sisters. Both had short blonde hair in the same bob style that Serena had noticed earlier at the farmhouse porch gathering. These girls' hair wasn't in ringlets however, but was instead parted in the middle and pulled straight out to the sides with ribbons. The rest of their hair was left to lie flat and was curled under at the ends. The girls wore identical dresses with a pattern containing various flowers

205

as well as what looked like a chicken motif. The dresses were pleated, had a zipper from waist to collar, featured an attached matching cloth belt, and were accented with short puffy sleeves. The girls were playing with chewing gum. They made long strings that they could wind and stretch into large loops that they pulled in and out of their mouths.

Serena and Jo smiled and nodded at the girls but quickened their pace before the girls took much notice of them. When they were a safe distance away, Serena asked, "Have you ever heard of the 'Monster Study'?"

"No? Should I have?"

"You may have studied it if you were a medical student, or as part of an ethics class."

"No on both of those. Does this have anything to do with the orphanage?"

Serena nodded. "This orphanage was a lab for human experiments."

Jo gasped.

"Wait, let me explain. The experiments were gentle and there were good intentions behind them. Speech pathologists from the University of Iowa tested a theory about why children stutter. The creator of the study, Dr. Wendell Johnson, was himself a stutterer. His goal was simply to gather information that could help children."

Jo gave her a quizzical look.

Serena continued. "His theory was that psychological pressure caused stuttering." She stopped to glance at the notes she'd loaded onto her pocket-sized digital notepad. "Johnson theorized, 'Stuttering begins in the ear of the listener, not in the mouth of the child.' Unfortunately the experimentation went

207

awry." She slipped the notepad back into her purse.

"With a name like the 'Monster Study' I assumed things went awry."

Serena plowed on, in a hurry to get through the material before they arrived at the orphanage. "Johnson's theory was so spot on that his research inadvertently caused stuttering in what had been perfectly normal children prior to the study. His theory was that all children struggle to speak. Overzealous parents and teachers make children so self-conscious and nervous that the children become sensitized to their speech and they then can't talk without stuttering."

Jo murmured, "I can see how that might happen."

"Johnson claimed that he owed his own stuttering to a first-grade teacher who misdiagnosed him as a stutterer. She had told his parents. His parents then constantly corrected him, which created the problem: the more he tried to speak correctly, the worse he stuttered." Serena pulled her digital notepad back out. "I like this quote by Johnson, 'The affliction is caused by the diagnosis.' The research bore out his theory but several of the orphans were damaged by the study."

Jo clucked her tongue. "That's a shame. What does this have to do with why we're here though?"

Serena smiled. "Ah, I'm getting to that. Johnson's peers warned him not to disclose the research because of the unfortunate timing of the study. It had ended right around the time that the world learned of Nazi medical experiments on living subjects, yi yi yi! He didn't publish the study. So, the orphans didn't know what had been done to them. But of course all things come out in the wash and the study was eventually found out."

"And what does this have to do with why those two men were here? And if they were already at the orphanage, aren't we too late? Why are we going there now?"

"They are covering something up. We went back further in time—they haven't been here yet. We're going back to get what they were covering up."

Jo snickered. "Sorry, I did it again---too many questions at once. Let's back up. What are they covering up?"

Serena sat down on a city bench. She touched through the windows on her notepad until she found the audio file of the men's conversation. "Listen for yourself."

Jo discretely inserted the earbud into her ear and arranged her red locks over it to obscure the futuristic gadget. She listened to the entire conversation, but only the middle part was of interest.

Voice 1: "We need to get it before she sees us."

Voice 2: "The Annie Wittenmyer Home is not far. We'll make it."

Voice 1: "It's not called that yet. Before 1949 it was the Iowa Soldiers' Orphans' Home."

Voice 2: "I don't want a history lesson."

Voice 1: "I can't have you stumbling around looking for The Annie Wittenmyer Home that doesn't exist yet."

Voice 2: "You're not coming?"

Voice 1: "We can't both prowl around the orphanage. Get in there, get it, and then come back here."

Voice 2: "They'll see one man as easily as two."

Voice 1: "Make sure that they don't."

Jo listened to the recording until the end but found nothing else worthwhile. "This doesn't say much."

211

"I could deduce the rest. The study went under the radar for so long that the details are probably a bit sketchy. The orphanage was accustomed to graduate students working with the kids. Wouldn't it be easy to slip in there and add one more experiment?"

"Ah, they want data for time travel?"

"As it was explained to me, we can only go back about one hundred years. What if we went into the past to find subjects who could give us access to a point further back in time than is accessible with the data we've already collected? Theoretically we could go back further and further into the past to open the window for time travel wider and wider. Well, not 'we', 'they'. Whoever is doing this."

"Why would they want to do this though? And why not go through proper channels? And…" Jo stopped herself before she piled on too many questions.

"I don't know and I don't know. That's the part I'm hoping we'll figure out after we find whatever it is that they went back to retrieve."

"So you're thinking that they've been here before?"

"No. Whoever they work for has been here before, or his previous minions have. But our two men weren't familiar with this place. I don't think they've been here before. They used a GPS to find the Blackhawk Hotel."

"Their boss left something behind, something incriminating?"

"That's my guess." Serena stood up. "Let's try to find it, shall we?"

"And our cover story is…?"

"We're from the University of Iowa and we're following up on the study that was conducted a few months ago."

213

"That'll work. Oh, another thing... You remember that I am a linguist? I noticed that the two men had an accent."

"Where are they from?"

Jo shook her curly red head. "That's the thing. I have no idea."

18

Serena and Jo arrived at the orphanage without further incident. The streets near the building were deserted. They arrived at the door and decided that the direct approach was best. Serena knocked on the door.

A small boy wearing pants that were cuffed at the ankles in a giant roll, a hand-me-down from a much older and taller child, opened the door. He said not a word as he opened the door wide enough for them to enter. Serena recognized instantly what the men were here to retrieve, as it was sitting not more than a few feet from the door---but it wasn't an object. "It" referred to what some in the espionage business called "the package". The package was a person. And that person was Eduardo. Eduardo pressed his index finger to his lips and gestured for them to "shoo".

Serena backed out the door, causing Jo to stumble. She marched onward toward the street. Jo followed suit. When the orphanage faded from view Jo rasped, "What's going on?"

Serena stopped. "Didn't you see Eduardo in there?"

"What? No, I didn't get close enough to see inside. What do you mean that Eduardo was in there?"

"I mean that Eduardo was in there! He was sitting inside. He motioned for me to stay quiet and leave, so I did."

"Wow."

"Yeah, I know. Well, this confirms that I was right about what they wanted. Eduardo is a data retrieval specialist. He can get what they want and program the bands, no problem."

"You don't think he's working for them?"

"No. He was scared."

Jo scratched her arm. "You don't think that he's nervous about the paradox issue, could that be all that he's worried about?"

"No, he was plenty anxious, as if he expected someone to kill all of us if we were caught there."

"Oh." Jo scratched her arm again.

Serena squinted at the red claw marks on her skin. "Why are you scratching so

217

much? You're going to make yourself bleed."

"I get hives when I'm nervous."

"There's good reason to be nervous. If Eduardo is here, in 1939, then who is Estep's team picking up? The Eduardo from before he got here, or the Eduardo from after? My mind is blown."

"When did Beav program us to return? Are we coming back at the same hour we left, or what?"

Serena grinned. "Hey, I just thought of something! Ruby Red and the past me will be turning up tomorrow, as in 1939's tomorrow, here."

"So? You can meet up with your own self!" Jo scratched her arm.

Serena tapped her hand. "Stop doing that. Don't worry, I don't mean me. What if *you* stay overnight and meet me tomorrow?"

"Where would I stay? Why would I do this?"

"Because you can tell everyone what happened. The extraction team will be here, remember? And they'll have those two men in custody. They can pick up Eduardo."

"Why don't we just go back right now and tell them? Why should I stay in 1939 overnight if I don't have to?"

Serena looked at her thoughtfully. "I hear what you're saying, but I have a gut feeling that we shouldn't leave here without him. If you don't want to stay on and wait for the team, we'd better go get him now."

Jo shook her red mane. "Just the two of us? We don't have any weapons. And if we did, would we know how to use them?"

"I have my tranquilizer gun right here in my purse. Estep threatened to take it away from me but he forgot. And before

219

you ask, yes, I know how to use it. I'm a pretty decent shot. I got a two-in-one last time."

"You don't strike me as a violent person."

"I'm not—this is only as a last resort, and it's not going to harm anybody unless they hit their head on the way down."

"Hmmm. How about we spend a few minutes coming up with a plan?"

Serena agreed. "I could get used to having help. You're right. I'll think before rushing in."

"Should we get a bite to…"

"Got it!"

"Got it?"

"The plan. I know what we should do."

Jo dug at her arm. "But you haven't even started thinking about it yet."

"Sure I have. You have your wristband and we have Ruby Red. We

220

don't need both. Leave me here—I have the means to get back. I want to keep a watch on him. Time travel or no, I'm not sure we can figure out what to do if he turns up missing. I'm already confused."

"Your plan is to watch the orphanage while I go get help? It's a good plan. I'll do it."

"Wait!" Serena pulled Jo's arm and led her behind a clump of trees. Voices came nearer and nearer until they were close enough to identify who they belonged to. She whispered, "We're too late. Go! Go!"

19

S erena in real time, present day, was startled to see Jo walking toward Ruby Red's GSI launch pad. "Has Beav sent you to assist me?" She was preparing to go back to Davenport, Iowa—completely unaware that she had *already been* on the mission to follow up on the conversation she had bugged at the Pompeian Room of the Blackhawk Hotel. She had *already been* to the Iowa Soldiers' Orphans' Home. Jo had

223

traveled slightly back in time to tell the crew what happened, and to catch Serena before she left. Serena had no clue that she had ever traveled with Jo, while Jo was experiencing déjà vu, having just left Serena in Iowa. While Serena was refreshed and eager to go, Jo was exhausted and not looking forward to the mission to retrieve "the other" Serena from 1939.

Jo scratched her arm.

"What have you done to your arm? You've clawed yourself until you've bled!" Serena gasped.

"I get hives when I'm nervous."

"Well, stop it. It makes me think of mosquito bites. Besides, even though time travel is intimidating, I think you'll find it worth facing up to your fears."

Jo said quietly, "I've already been." She had fretted about how she would tell Serena about the failed time travel mission, and how Jo had left Serena back in Davenport, Iowa 1939. There seemed no words for this particular announcement. She decided to let Serena figure it out for herself, which gratefully didn't take her long.

Serena studied her face. "Uh oh. We've already gone to the past and back, haven't we?" Her dark hair fell into her line of vision and for once she didn't bother to tuck the stubborn locks behind her ears. She stood still, peeking out at Jo from behind her hair.

Jo looked away. She couldn't quite face up to the cowardly actions she had taken. Surely there could have been a way to stay there and help? Jo wasn't convinced that leaving her there was the only option. And yet, Serena was the senior time traveler on the project. Jo reassured herself that she had done the best she could.

225

"Oh." Serena blinked. "I'm still back there aren't I?"

Jo stammered, "I-I'm sorry. I should have stayed. I'm not sure how all of this works. Can we go back and save you? I feel horrible for leaving you there."

Serena gulped. "Did I die?"

Jo's eyes flew open wide. "No! No! I most certainly hope---No. You were fine when I left, but you're in danger. I came back to get help, as you asked me to do, and to warn you."

"What kind of danger?"

"I can explain once we're there. The crew decided that we should go back to Davenport about an hour before the incident, to give us time to get our plans in place. But we have to go right away. We can't risk that something is happening to you in 1939 *right now*. We don't know enough about this time travel technology to know if we can reverse a... situation."

"I suppose that they are insisting on backup?" Serena sighed. That meant that she would be working with Agent Estep. There was something about working with him that brought out the worst in her.

"Oh yes. They're suiting up." Jo tried to see beyond the glare of GSI's exterior glass windows for signs that the team inside was ready.

"OK then, let's go." She pulled her hair back away from her face and bound it with a ponytail ring. She figured that there was no point in waiting for the crew. They'd turn up soon enough. She hoped to get back there ahead of Estep.

"Serena?" Jo reached out and tugged on her green scarf.

"Yes?"

"Your other self has a tranquilizer gun." Jo had an idea, but she hoped not to have to explain it. She had rehearsed in her head how to tell Serena her plan. If she

227

had to say it aloud it would sound even more awful than it had inside her head.

Serena patted the hip-hugging bag strapped to her waist. "Oh. Yes, I suppose so. It's in my purse, and my 'other self' has my purse too." Her contemporary purse had been slender enough to slip under her old-fashioned dress when returning to 1939. "Anyway, apparently she does have the gun. Why are you asking me this?"

Jo continued to speak at a lower volume than she usually did. "I don't know how we're going to coordinate you not seeing, well, you." She said this pointedly, to prompt Serena to connect the dots on her own.

Serena looked for Jo's facial expression to reveal what secrets she wasn't spilling. She was drawing a blank. "Why not just leave me here so that I can't see my other self? I don't understand why I'm going back to investigate what happened to myself. This is silly, even for me. I mean, of course I want to do it, but I'm surprised that anyone else wants me to. This is the sort of thing that people usually forbid me to do. Aren't we still worried about the grandfather paradox thing?"

Jo glanced at the GSI doors and saw shadowy figures moving around. "I think they're almost ready. Bottom line, you deserve the best detective on this case, and that's you. I fought for your right to come."

Serena mulled it over. "I see. Well, as much as I appreciate that, I know we have to tread carefully. Your solution is to tranquilize me, I mean the 'other' me?"

"Yes. I need the version of you who's standing in front of me, so I thought you could use your second gun, the one you have on you to..."

"You want me to shoot my*self*?"

Jo scratched her arm.

229

Serena grimaced. "Stop doing that."

"That's what the other you said." Jo stopped scratching. "So, do you think you can do it?"

"I can do it. Estep threatened to take that gun away from me but he forgot. And before you ask, yes, I know how to use it. I'm a pretty decent shot. I got a…"

"Two-for-one. Yes, I know."

Serena exhaled noisily. "My other self stole my story. I guess she's got it coming."

"Good to see you've kept your sense of humor."

"Always. When you asked about the other me having the tranquilizer gun, is it because you're afraid she'll shoot me first?" Serena laughed.

"No, I was wondering if the other you could defend yourself." Jo added, "Should you call your husband before we go?"

Serena stared at her. "It's that serious? I should say good-bye? What would happen if the me in 1939 died? Wouldn't I be OK? 1939 wasn't on my timeline—it was way before I was born."

Beav yelled from across the landing pad. "Hey, they're not ready. Wait!"

Serena frowned. "He caught us. I wanted to get back there ahead of them."

Jo shrugged. "Sorry, but it's for the best. We need them."

Beav jogged over to where they were. "You two looked like you were having an intense conversation. What did I miss?"

Jo answered, "We were wondering what would happen to Serena if the other version of herself died in 1939."

Beav ruminated, paced with his arms clasped behind his back, and ruminated some more. "If we are in a closed timeline curve, it's like walking in a circle. These things, like the death of your other self, can't happen because it would make free will null and void. We aren't allowed to reverse the order of things, unless we delved into predestination and the concept that all events are preordained. If all of time and space are ordered by predestination and not free will, then we're in a possible quandary. There may be no hard and fast rules if the universe is governed by predestination, as there would be no logical contradiction to prevent us from tampering with our own lives. What's one random string of events compared to another? Predestination implies only that the order of things was chosen ahead of time, but there's no qualifier to indicate that this particular order, or even the events themselves, is of any significance to a Higher Power, or to anyone else, or to any*thing* else. Without the concept of free will, does it matter if you die before you were even born? Does it matter if you exist at all?"

Serena shook her head like a dog might do after getting his fur wet. "I don't think I absorbed much of what you said. What does free will have to do with it? I take it that I should be hoping that we all have free will. If so, I'm not worried. I believe that God gives us free will, there's no doubt in my mind. That's settled. Let's go."

Beav balked. "Free will implies that you have a choice about your future. That's why the you that's stuck in 1939 can't die. If you die, you can't live out the free will choices that you made after you were born. Say for example that you decided to go to college. If you erased yourself, you'd erase the decision you made to go to college, because there would be no you to go. Nullifying free will is forbidden, if indeed free will exists. But since the past you is outside of your personal timeline, i.e. before you were born, this conversation is moot. How can you erase yourself by dying in 1939?"

"Sometimes I think you talk just to amuse yourself." Serena folded her arms across her chest. "That scenario only applies if the past me was prevented from being born, right? This is different. There are two versions of myself because the other me has gone back in time before my own lifetime even began."

Beav rubbed his chin, "I don't know how that ties into my musings about free will."

"It doesn't!" Serena continued, "Couldn't she, the me that is stuck in 1939, theoretically die without her demise having any effect on me? She's off my personal timeline altogether. I think she's an extra, like a clone. She could vanish, what would it hurt? As long as the 1939 me doesn't alter history for other people, I don't see how it would be a problem if she lived or died in 1939 while I'm perfectly fine here, right now, standing in front of you." Serena pondered this and added, "Then again, maybe if she dies I'll just vanish, like a vapor. Here today, gone tomorrow. My free will wouldn't have been established yet. So, basically, Beav, I don't think anything you said answers the question or even comes close to answering it. Let's operate on the assumption that if I die in 1939 it could be a very bad thing." Serena heaved a sigh. "What's taking the crew so long?"

As if on cue, they appeared. Ruby Red and the crew, including Agent Estep and his team, traveled to Davenport, Iowa 1939, materializing a few yards from the Ruby Red that the "other Serena" had arrived in earlier. Beav had programmed the new Ruby Red to emerge a safe distance from itself, but it was still startling to see two of them side-by-side. The crew stood around for a few seconds, staring with wonder at the identical time machines.

Serena asked, "What happens if I use the other Ruby Red and my other self uses this one? If we mix things up will we cause an implosion?"

Agent Estep walked to where Serena was standing and squatted down to bring his face closer to her level. When he was meeting her eyeball to eyeball he said, "You have to take this seriously. You aren't dying on my watch. If you smart off, spin your musings, or spark your own crazy plan I'll take you out."

Serena backed away. "Got it. But don't worry, I'm taking myself out."

Jo stepped up to the plate to explain. "She's going to shoot her other self with the tranquilizer gun. Then we can pull that version of Serena out and send her home."

Estep grunted. His face turned an alarming shade of crimson and then nearly purple. His crew cut had grown out enough that a carpet of dark curls sprang from his head as he pounded the ground in a circular path around Jo and Serena. He was like a lion in a cage, a hungry and pissed off lion.

The lion stopped. He bellowed, "That's the kind of stupid crazy-ass plan that I was talking about! You're OUT!"

Jo spoke with quiet confidence. "It was my plan."

Beav snapped his fingers. "Hey, focus. We are down to forty minutes before this thing goes down. Sorry, Jo, I agree with Estep on this one. The idea of Serena shooting her other self is a shockingly bad plan. I wish that Serena wasn't here at all. I have to admit that I echo Estep's concerns, although I wouldn't have put it the way that he did."

Serena swallowed hard. "Are you two done talking to me, and about me, as if I were a child? Brief me on this operation so that we can all go home."

Estep clapped his large hands so effectively that the sound reverberated over the corn field. "Gather round people!"

Beav took over. "All right, here's the status of what we know, and more importantly what we don't know. Jo and Serena were investigating the Iowa Soldiers' Orphans' Home, which is, or was, the destination of the two mystery men who used our own wristbands to travel. Let me remind you, these bands were killed for. We've lost two of our people already. Whoever these men are, they are involved in the murders of two of our own crew. And furthermore they are working for someone bigger than themselves, so keep that in mind as well. We don't know

238

how many of them might pop up, and we have no idea who they are."

Jo continued, "But before I left Serena stranded, I did hear the voices of the people coming toward us, toward her. And that's what freaked me out the most."

Beav held up his hands. "Wait, let's think this through before the big reveal. It doesn't mean that these people are traitors. What it means is that there is something going on that we don't yet understand. Jo told me who she heard, and it doesn't make sense. This has become a challenging puzzle that Serena should be involved in, especially as it concerns her life. We don't know what will happen to her—to you, Serena—if she is left to die in 1939. That's why she's here. But bringing her here to save her own self is a conundrum."

Jo said, "We have only thirty-five odd minutes left so I'll spill it: I heard Malirah Cravitz and James Edison Spector, I know

239

it. I also caught a glimpse of Malirah's shoes. She has a penchant for custom-made outrageously-high boots. She's a personal friend of mine. Believe me when I say that it was her."

Serena digested this stunning revelation at lightning speed. "A shocker for sure, but why am I in grave danger? I'd hardly think of James as an imposing threat. I bet I could take him even without my tranquilizer gun. As for Malirah, I can't see her hurting anyone. There has to be an explanation for what they're doing here. They're probably working on a future mission."

Jo cleared her throat. "Except that they were with someone else." She paused. "They were with Jorgi Gorantisch. I'd know his voice anywhere."

Serena was without words for a microsecond. "But he's…"

"Dead," said a voice that no one was expecting.

Natalie Buske Thomas

20

Ann Kinji redirected the interrogations after Beav and Agent Estep flew out of GSI on what they declared to be a Code Red. She didn't know why they felt the need to go back to Davenport with Serena, and she didn't care at the moment. What it meant was that she and Lehman would plow through the large number of witnesses and suspects on their own, at least until more of the core team showed

243

up. She had instructed Ruby to hold down the fort for five minutes while she and Lehman regrouped. The two were in her office, draining a cup of coffee and strategizing how to proceed with fewer people than anticipated.

Lehman clucked his tongue and wagged his head. "You'd think with time travel we wouldn't have time crunch issues."

Ann echoed the sentiment. "I'm not sure that Beav's COT protocol is the way to go."

"Oh, I have to agree with Beav on that. I don't have to like it, but it's solid theory."

"Explain it to me. I must confess that I often skim his memos."

Lehman smirked. Beav had a fondness for spitting out batches of memos at odd hours; most of his messages were time-stamped between midnight and 3:00AM.

Lehman remembered the memo about COT because the concept had intrigued him. "I'll pull up Beav's exact message. It'll only take me a second. Yep, here it is:

'Hey, this is Beav thinking outside of the box again. I came up with COT, good for a rest but not for a slumber. COT is an acronym for Convenient Optimized Time protocol. All bands will be programmed for optimal results. Why blindly return at the exact instant of departure? Humans need time to absorb their thoughts and reactions. COT default programming will be sixty minutes later than the departure time unless requested otherwise.'

That's all he says about it, but I have to agree. There's no need for the return to be instantaneous with the departure. It's confusing, wouldn't you say? My brain can't wrap itself around the concept yet. Until time travel feels like a mundane mode of transportation, isn't it best to operate within the confines of what we know—and simulate a plane schedule?"

Ann swooped up a pencil and tapped the eraser on the rim of her empty coffee mug without tipping it over. Tapping the eraser instead of chewing on it was her step-down to quitting pencils altogether. "You know me. I'm ready for instant travel. I'd prefer that they go back in time and arrive before they departed. Color me impatient."

Lehman grinned. "You've established that you're not a fan of COT. It is what it is though. How do you want to handle these interrogations now that we're even more short-staffed?"

"While it goes against my nature, I'm leaning toward waiting until two or more of the crew show. I'm tired, Lehman. I thought I would have sent you home to Texas by now, and yet here you sit. GSI has barely opened its doors and already we

are derailed by an unexpected investigation
that has nothing to do with issues that GSI
was designed to investigate. Once again,
corruption from within has interfered with
getting the real work done. How is this
different from the Presidency?"

"I've been meaning to ask. How is
Joe, I mean Mr. President Smythe, doing?
Yours are hard shoes to fill. His feet can't
possibly fit into those things." Lehman
glanced at Ann's tiny feet and laughed at
his own joke. "Does he keep you in the
loop?"

"You know, I only hear from Joe
about oh, every hour on the hour. He's
inventing any reason he can think of to
contact me, and he's not even bothering to
be creative with his excuses."

"Does this have to do with our Irish
time traveler?"

"It has everything to do with Jo. I've
said it before, but I'll say it again. America

doesn't want a bachelor president. He's pathetic, mooning and moping. He needs to get on with it and marry the girl."

"Oh I don't know, half of America will be heartbroken when Mr. President is taken."

"When the president makes the tabloids more often than any real source of news, it's time to get the man a ring."

Ruby rapped on the door. "It's been ten minutes. Is there a change of plan that I should know about?"

"Sorry Ruby, I should have told you that we were wearing down. We're waiting for reinforcements." Ann met Ruby at the door. "Can you hold down the fort a while longer?"

Ruby shook her head. "No need. Your people are here. I have five team members waiting for you in the lobby. Two of them have asked to speak to you privately. Should I send them up?"

"Of course." Ann turned to Lehman, "You know what this is about?"

Lehman shook his head. "Not at all."

Ruby disappeared, leaving the door slightly ajar.

Natalie Buske Thomas

21

"Malirah?" Jo didn't know whether to greet her friend or flee from her.

Malirah spoke quickly. "Before this gets any more carried away, listen up. Serena is not in any danger; stand down. You do have to get her out of there though before she blows our cover." Malirah stepped the rest of the way out from the corn field, from the spot a few rows back where James Edison had programmed for

251

her to appear. They thought it best that she have the element of surprise in her favor, in case Estep's team was trigger happy.

"Your cover?" Serena pressed.

Malirah shook a long manicured nail at her and made a *tsk, tsk* sound. "Need to know basis. I can't say anything with the extraction team listening. I came from GSI directly here, to stop you from messing things up. I have a note from Ms. Ann Kinji herself."

Malirah held up a one-sentence scrawl in Kinji's distinctive large-looped cursive, written with a pressure point so hard that the imprint could have embossed an entire pad of paper: "Get Serena out of there now—mission aborted." The note contained the raised seal of the President of the United States. Apparently even the President takes office supplies when leaving a job.

Estep gestured for his team. "Get Serena, fast and clean." His team darted toward Serena, who let out a small shriek, covered her face, and cowered.

"No, you idiots! The *other* Serena, the one outside the orphanage. This is what I get when working with the B-Team."

"Why didn't you bring your guys?" asked Serena, trying not to take it personally that her life was worth only a B-Team rescue.

"They had to return to an official operation that I had been scheduled to lead, you know, in the real world where not every mission involves playing a game of 'fetch Serena'."

Estep gave the extraction team their final orders. "No one can see you. Don't hurt her, but make sure she's quiet." He called after them, "If it's a choice between keeping her quiet and not hurting her, use the tranquilizer gun."

Jo adopted a smug expression. "Well, well. My idea wasn't so ridiculous after all." Her curls often accentuated her mood; as she moved her head her hair seemed alive. At this moment her hair danced and jeered.

Estep's own black curls were tightly woven in comparison and if they ever danced, it was against his will. "What is ridiculous, Jo, is that you wanted Serena to shoot her own self. The ways in which that would have gone wrong would have cost me my…"

"Day job," said Beav, Serena and Jo in unison.

Estep's eyes flitted from Jo to Beav and then settled firmly on Serena. "Don't move. No, actually go back home. I want no risk of you seeing your other self."

Serena said, "I can't go home, because then how would my future self get here? Jo went back to before I launched, so the me in front of you right now is actually the me of slightly into the past."

Beav piped up. "I agree, but that doesn't matter. It's not good to have the two versions of you together. And it's best not to have both versions of the time machine here either. Paradox is a real concern."

"More importantly, I can't stomach seeing two Serenas at once." Estep's stance, his legs planted far apart and his right arm fully extended to the tip of his pointed index finger, expressed non-negotiation more effectively than anything he could have said.

Serena stood her ground. "I can't go until my other self does. If I leave now, ahead of her, then I'll already know what is happening right now, *before* I go with Jo to the orphanage. That would alter history even more, don't you think?"

"She has a good point," said Beav.

255

"She does? I'm so confused." Jo gave up trying to understand that particular puzzle and moved on to the logistics of getting back. "Should I leave now in Ruby Red so that there won't be two time machines here? Serena can take my wristband so that she can get back after her other self leaves in the second Ruby Red with *my* other self. Does that make sense?"

Beav nodded. "That will work."

Estep growled at Serena, "All right then, go hide in the corn and don't come out until you know that both time machines are gone."

It wasn't often that Serena swore. She was more comfortable using humor, especially sarcasm, to reflect her frustrations in life. So on the rare occasions when she let loose with a few choice cuss words it always surprised people. As she sulked her way over to the cornfield, where the mosquitos and the musky smell sucked her in, she surprised people with every word that she said.

22

Safely back at GSI, there was now only one Serena existing on the time curve—the real time, present day Serena. The timelines never did cross and the Serena stuck in 1939 seemed to have vanished. It was a question they would ask the GSI scientists about later, although Serena wasn't sure that she wanted to know what happened to the other version of herself. All in all, when setting aside the creepy notion that

259

the "other" Serena may have disintegrated, it had been an uneventful extraction. One of the B-Team agents had been lurking behind the tree line near the orphanage, in the spot where Jo had said that she and Serena would be. Since no passerby was around, he quietly spoke to the two women as soon as they saw him there.

"Agent Estep wants you back at Ruby Red." His uniform confirmed his identity and there was no reason to doubt him.

They followed him back to the cornfield. Serena and Jo left shortly thereafter via the remaining Ruby Red. Seconds later, Serena (the slightly-into-the-future-from-her-other-self version) used Jo's wristband to return. No paradox occurred and everyone breathed a sigh of relief. But there would be a long night ahead as they waited to secure the clearances necessary to hear Malirah's story.

Serena, just one person again, insisted that she be dismissed to go home. She hadn't seen Tom or the kids in what felt to her like months instead of hours. "I'm drained. I feel my life slipping through the sands of time."

Ann raised an eyebrow. "A bit dramatic wouldn't you say? Sure, go. We're stuck for a while anyway. In fact, everyone should go. Get some dinner. Feed the dog. Do whatever you do to unwind."

Everyone immediately shuffled toward the door. Ann shouted over the din, "Stop!" Everyone froze. "You aren't done for the day--- I can't hold all of these suspects for much longer. We have to arrest them or let them go. I expect to see all of you back here at 9:00PM. Malirah will brief us on whatever bombshell she's holding onto and then we'll attack that backlog of interrogations."

Serena started to speak but Ann anticipated her question and cut her off. "Sorry, Serena, that goes for you too."

Four hours later they all obediently returned to GSI, all but one. James Edison didn't make it back. They waited fifteen minutes for him. Finally they decided to proceed without him. Permission was granted to share top secret information with Ann, Serena, Jo, Lehman, Beav and Estep. All others were assigned to interrogation duties on the lower level of the building.

When Ann closed the door to her office, Serena asked Malirah, "Should we bring Eduardo up from interrogation? Where does he fit into all of this?"

Malirah thought it over. "Let's leave him where he is for now. He already knows what I'm about to say. You can talk to him when I'm done."

"Fair enough, please begin," said Ann.

"I was working with the CIA. I'm not CIA—I was only an asset. They recruited me after Eduardo became a whistleblower. He suspected that Jorgi was selling secrets and stealing technology. Eduardo insisted that the CIA not get directly involved and pleaded with them to use our own people as assets."

Serena made an attempt to whistle but fell short of the mark. "Oh ho! You're saying that he 'pleaded'. He didn't win the argument did he? So who's CIA among us?"

Malirah looked down at her long fingers. She seemed to be examining the intricate designs on her nails. She took a deep breath. "It's James Edison, and the late Gentry. Poor guy."

"So you really did know Gentry well enough to be rattled by his death. I knew it! You can't fake the look you had on your face when you saw him." Serena noticed

Estep's protest of her habit of interjecting herself into briefings. As if his moaning and groaning wasn't enough of a tip off, he upped his game by scraping his feet across the floor. "I'm sorry, Malirah, please continue." The floor scraping, groaning and moaning ceased. Serena knew that the ruckus would begin anew if she derailed the briefing again.

"Yes, I knew Gentry. We made up that backstory about the dialysis, living with his parents, all of it. He was far from sickly. He was at the prime of his life and he was really going places at the agency. What a shame. As for James Edison, he's not quite the star that Gentry was, but he's sharp in his own way. Obviously it doesn't look good for James. This isn't the kind of thing he'd miss."

Malirah paused but no one had anything to say. She continued. "Basically we were supposed to watch him. He wasn't doing anything that we could pin on him. It was like he knew he was being watched or something, we don't know why he stopped doing the things that Eduardo had found suspicious. James Edison and Gentry got impatient. They decided we should bait Jorgi.

So we did a test run with the wristbands, bringing Jorgi into the fold. We issued him a gag order to sell him on the concept that what we were doing was highly confidential, and only us four knew about it; Eduardo, James Edison, Gentry, and me; or us five if you want to include Jorgi in that count. It worked! We could tell that Jorgi was getting restless and he was on the phone more than usual."

Malirah stopped to drink a sip of water. She took a couple of deep breaths and then continued speaking. "Serena guessed right: Eduardo chose that location because of the 'Monster Study'. He had done a research paper about the stuttering experiments on orphans when he was a pre-med student. And yes, the potential was there to slip in without anyone suspecting that Eduardo wasn't another researcher from the university. Serena also got it right when she guessed that collecting brain data was the goal, but what she didn't know is that the goal was a hoax all along. It was only a story we told to Jorgi.

We thought he'd run straight to whoever he was selling us out to, and we were right. We knew he was reporting everything to someone. We went through with it. The five of us went to Davenport, Iowa 1939. Eduardo got himself into the orphanage. His role there was to conduct a survey, and as you know, Eduardo is a nondescript sort of man, the kind that people forget ever having seen. We knew he could get away with doing this without altering history. Jorgi didn't know what Eduardo was really doing in there—he thought Eduardo was collecting brain data from as many orphans as he could, for the reasons that Serena had deduced: a bigger time window for time travel into the past. Think of how valuable that could be to the right buyer! And it was a secret mission, known only to the five of us.

Well, do the math. Jorgi is dead. Gentry is dead. James is now missing. Eduardo was missing—how did you find him, and where was he?"

Ann answered, "We'll find that out next when we talk to him. I'm curious to know why Eduardo scheduled Serena's first test launch for Davenport 1939. Why would he risk a blown cover?"

"She wasn't supposed to be there at the same time that we were. Remember, she went back to 1939 at a slightly different time to follow a lead---the very

267

time window that we were there! The odds of that are slim, but then again we are talking about Serena who has a long history of stumbling into the heart of a mess that even time and space can't contain. She was brilliant to have figured out all of the things we were doing. I felt bad that she was chasing down a story that we concocted. I wanted to write her into the mission, but they told me no. Too many people were involved as is. Serena, I've followed your career since I was in junior high. You've been an inspiration to me, that women can excel in careers that are traditionally dominated by men."

Serena felt both flattered and old. She also didn't know what to say. Fortunately Jo jumped in to save the day. "Serena's work on the hoax end of this was minimal. She was making good progress on the real case behind the cover story. In fact, she may have saved your life, Malirah. If not for her getting involved, where would you be right now? Not here at GSI with us! You'd be an easy target at home. Would anyone else have thought to bug the conversation that those two men were having? I heard them talking and I'm not sure I would have thought to record what…"

"I've got it!" Serena yelped. "Jo, how good of a linguist are you?"

Jo blushed. "I'm brilliant to be honest."

"And yet you couldn't place the odd accent that you said the men had, right? To me it sounded American, but I know what you mean, that it was slightly off."

"Right. It's not an American accent. It's not an acting or forced accent, and I don't believe that these men had learned English as a second language. This is a puzzle. I've never run across this before."

269

Serena leapt out of her seat. "Exactly! It's because it hasn't happened yet. Those two men were from the future. That would explain why they sound like Americans, but not quite, as if the language and culture has evolved; or will evolve, since we're talking about the future."

Estep snorted. "If you're done spinning theories that we can't prove, can we bring Eduardo in here?"

Malirah agreed. "I don't have anything more to say. Eduardo will be able to provide more insight."

Serena clapped her hands together suddenly, making several of them jump. "Hey, since we're waiting anyway, what do you say to a short trip to and from the landing pad?

Estep's eyes narrowed. "Does this short trip include a much longer trip through time and space?"

"Why yes it does!" Serena pointed to Beav. "You can tweak the programming fast if I'm only asking you to do a few adjustments, right?"

"Theoretically I can. Where do you want to go?"

"I want to meet Albert Einstein. And I want to bring our young friend Nicholas with me. He's a big fan of Einstein and I promised."

Beav clucked his tongue. "First of all, you shouldn't have promised him anything. Secondly, I have no idea where to place you for that. And last, I can't make you invisible. You can't meet Einstein without altering history. Short answer—no."

Serena was quick to reply, which raised the crew's suspicion that she had been waiting for the first idle moment to "spontaneously" pitch the Einstein visit. "I know where to find him. He was at the Metropolitan Opera House on December

21, 1930. He saw 'Carmen' on that date. We wouldn't be noticed among all of those people attending the opera, so there's no need to worry about us altering history."

Beav said, "They won't let you in without a ticket."

Serena gave her rebuttal. "No need. Einstein was invited backstage after the show. We can wait outside the opera house to catch a glimpse of him. See? I research things from time to time. I even found a photo in the AP archives. Oh come on, what do you say? We owe Nicholas an Einstein sighting for all the work he did for us during Operation Covert Coffee. He's not going to talk to Einstein or anything, just see him from afar."

23

No one was surprised when Serena got her way. The crew watched her walk toward the landing pad where Nicholas was already waiting, confirmation that Serena had indeed intended all along to spring this Einstein visit on Beav at the first opportunity. Furthermore, she had been apparently quite confident that he would agree to it.

This time they skipped traveling by Ruby Red, upon Beav's insistence that he would program the bands and that's it. Serena was agreeable to that, knowing that she had treaded upon Beav's good nature enough. They were hurried. Even though the time travel itself would cost them nothing at all, the prep to and from was in real time. So without her typical dramatic exit Serena left present day for December 21, 1930.

She and Nicholas were easily swallowed up by a crowd, so much so that they feared that they wouldn't be able to see Einstein when he came out. They figured they could squeeze through to get a better look when he emerged.

While they waited for Einstein to appear, Serena indirectly asked Nicholas why he wanted to see Einstein. She made suppositions. "You admire another genius like yourself? He was homeschooled too. I suppose you have a lot in common with him."

Nicholas shrugged.

"That's not it?"

"Not really."

Serena was persistent. "Then why do you want to see him?" Seconds passed. Nicholas' face was blank. Either he was thinking or he was tuning her out. She tried again. "Why do you admire him?"

"I like what he says."

"Ah." Serena stamped her feet to try to warm up her toes. "You mean about relativity and science?" Nicholas said nothing. She didn't give up. "Can you give me an example?"

"He said that he has only two rules for conduct. 'The first is: have no rules. The second is: be independent of the opinion of others.'"

"I see. You side with Americans from the 30's who admired Einstein as a rugged

275

individualist who was doing his own thing."

"Not everybody liked him, Ms. Wilcox."

"True. But you admire him."

"I have an Einstein quote on the wall in my room. 'Try not to become a man of success, but rather a man of value.'"

"Ah. So you like his integrity then?"

Nicholas muttered what sounded like agreement.

Serena's patience for navigating through a conversation with a teenage boy had limited reserves. She was relieved to see that the doors were opening. "There he is!"

She and Nicholas weaved through the crowd. Serena let Nicholas bolt ahead to get as close as he could. The boy was tall and slim, and because he was a teenager, no one gave him a second look. He was dressed for the time period, but upon closer inspection he wouldn't have fit in, especially if he had spoken to anyone. American English had evolved a great deal since the 1930's. He would have been feared as a foreigner of unknown origin. Besides the way he sounded, the way he smelled could have aroused curiosity. Nicholas was drenched in Old Spice body wash that he hadn't fully rinsed off of his skin during his hasty attempt at a shower. Thankfully Nicholas made it through the crowd and back to where Serena was standing without anyone hearing or smelling anything awry.

He was beaming. "I saw him!"

Serena had caught a glimpse of Einstein too. He was wearing a black tux with a bow tie. His hair really did look as wild and rumpled as caricaturists made it out to be. His dark mustache was a hairy caterpillar on his upper lip. But it was his raised eyebrows that amused her most of all. The woman on his arm was stunning, what Serena could see of her anyway. There was a definite downside to being a short person. The din from the crowd had given them anonymity, but now people were beginning to disperse. They couldn't risk being overheard speaking in their futuristic American tongue so Serena gestured to her band without speaking. Nicholas nodded that he understood. The two of them returned to the landing pad.

Beav was standing in the same spot where they left him, given that no time had passed. He said, "What do you have in your hand? Is that a playbill? You said you weren't going in."

Serena sniffed. "I found this on the sidewalk. Someone must have dropped it. I picked it up as a souvenir for Nicholas." She handed it to him.

"Not signed by Einstein I hope." Beav was only half joking.

"Of course not! We were in and out of 1930 without anyone seeing us. But that would have been amazing if we could have gotten Albert Einstein's autograph."

"Then I'm glad you didn't think of it. Nicholas, it's always good to see you, but we must bid you adieu. Eduardo is on his way, they buzzed me."

Eduardo arrived at the briefing shortly after Beav and Serena had returned to the room. The sight of him took them aback. He was a beaten man, physically and spiritually. He was but a shell of his former self, and he hadn't been big to begin with.

He spoke barely above a whisper. "I can't tell you much. I didn't see anyone's faces—they put a bag over my head. Contrary to how it appears, they didn't harm me in any way. The injuries you're looking at are self-inflicted, due to not

279

being able to see. I fell several times while making my escape."

Ann looked at Estep. "What's this about an escape? I thought he gave you the address to pick him up?"

Estep replied, "He was on his knees outside of the complex when we got to him. He said that his captors had left him alone and that he'd gotten out. We checked the place out but they had swept it clean. No trace, no DNA, nothing to work off of. If these men are from the future, their DNA wouldn't be in the system anyway."

Serena couldn't let this opportunity pass. "You've adopted my theory then, about the men being from the future?"

Agent Estep ignored her.

Eduardo nodded. "I'd have to say that she's on the right track." He swallowed hard and adjusted his shoulders. "I have to confess something. It shames me to have to admit it, but Malirah is wrong about the fabrication. I didn't want to tell her the truth: my work with the CIA included that I actually follow through with collecting the data from the orphans, and for that I know that there is a dark mark on my soul. And yes, whoever they are, they have this new data—I can confirm that Jorgi managed to get his hands on it. On a positive note, we too have this same wider time travel window, as I retained my own copy of the data I retrieved from the Iowa mission."

Eduardo continued. "I'm sorry I can't offer you anything more about the identity of the people we are dealing with. All I ever knew is that Jorgi was selling our technology to someone, and that he was definitely interested in the test launch. I expected the CIA to catch him before anything bad happened. Had I known that everything would go haywire I'd have come straight to you, Madam President."

Ann corrected him, "It's not Madam President anymore."

Eduardo tipped his head to the side. "It was back then."

Ann perked up. "Are you saying that we've been on the right track all along? Evidently we were working Project Scarecrow and we didn't even know it."

Eduardo slowly nodded his head. "And by 'Project Scarecrow', you are referring to your investigation into how time-travel technology has been compromised, correct?"

Ann said, "That's that whole purpose of founding GSI. Why else would I be looking into it?"

Beav made an attempt to be helpful. "Well, you've given our mission the same name as the scientists' original project so it's unclear."

Ann didn't respond.

Eduardo moved on with his train of thought. "They, whoever they are, needed an inside man and got one with Jorgi. You're right—this isn't an internal affairs situation. Jorgi was never truly one of us. Rest assured, we're the good guys. But Project Scarecrow fears are valid; there's something ominous on the loose. When you launched the Gödel Solution Institute I felt it was an answer to prayer. Finally we were hearing from a Higher Power: time and space was not without justice."

He continued, even though his voice was now so weak that they had to strain to hear him. "When you selected Project Scarecrow as your first investigation into the ethics of science and technology, I was both honored and terrified. I had already agreed to work with the CIA before I got word that you were involved. When you took on Project Scarecrow, while I was

283

immensely relieved that help was forthcoming, I didn't know if I should break protocol. I decided to trust the system and keep my agreement with the CIA. I'm truly sorry. I thought I had made the right decision."

Ann patted him gently on the hand. "You've beat yourself up enough. We still don't know who we are dealing with. We might not have handled it any better. Is there ever any point in looking back?"

Serena was quick to offer up her musings. "There's always value in analyzing the past, remembering it, and piecing it together with the present and the future. Solving a puzzle relies on building upon the pieces that have already been put together. That's how we know where the next pieces go. I also think of it as…"

Lehman spoke for the first time since the briefing had commenced. His tone had an uncharacteristically sharp edge to it. "It was a rhetorical question." He felt all eyes on him. "Sorry, I know I'm stealing Estep's thunder in being the one to rein Serena in, but we all know that someone has to do it or we'll be here all night." He sighed and stretched his long legs. "Don't mind me, I'm irritable because I'm exhausted and I miss my wife."

Serena had been working something out in her head while Lehman was talking. She was oblivious to the fact that he was talking about her, as her own thoughts had drowned out his voice almost immediately. She put the investigation back into play. "Eduardo, why did the men leave you alone? What scared them off?"

"When my phone rang they wanted me to answer it. I spoke in code so I don't think it was my message that tipped them off."

Serena considered another possibility. "Is there any possibility that the caller ID is what spooked them?"

Eduardo sat up straight. "Yes!" He chuckled. "Mandolin Fredrik was *their* guy. Jorgi had hired him. If Mandolin's number was on my phone, it could only mean one thing—that Mandolin was working against them, and had probably gone straight to you, which is exactly what happened."

Serena rubbed her hands together. "Now we're getting somewhere! Bring Mandolin in."

Ann considered this. "Are you sure you want him in here? We can interrogate him with the others."

Beav asserted, "He made himself a good guy, at least somewhat, when he dropped off that phone. He deserves to be heard."

Ann gestured for Estep to go. While they waited for him to return with

Mandolin, she asked Eduardo if he had any other information that could help them with the investigation. He offered up what he knew. Most of it was intelligence that they had already figured out on their own, but one nugget was golden.

"I know where they're going next," Eduardo said. Everyone leaned forward to hear his weak voice. "They did get me to program the bands for them before I escaped. I'll program your remaining bands to the same frequency so that you can send someone in. I'm sorry. I didn't want to do it. I was too cowardly to die for the cause." He blanched. "I-I thought I could hold out. I wanted to be a man who would never sell out his country, more importantly his ethics. The power of this technology is a priceless treasure that I wanted to guard with my life. I failed as a scientist, as an ethical human being, and as a man."

Estep had returned with Mandolin in cuffs and had caught the end of Eduardo's pitiful speech. He said, "Get the man some bacon." No one knew quite what he meant by that, but all of them assumed that Eduardo's open vulnerability made Estep squirm. He assisted Mandolin into a chair and then slid his own chair close to Mandolin, in case he should try any sudden moves. Estep explained, unnecessarily, "Better safe than sorry."

"Indeed," said Ann, disregarding that Estep was trying to make up for not having secured Eduardo in cuffs before the hospital fiasco. It would have been more difficult for Mandolin to have snatched him if Eduardo had been restrained. *Water under the bridge*, she told herself. "He's all yours, Serena."

Serena dove in. "Mandolin, I've heard a lot about you. We know that Jorgi hired you to work against us, but you have since then, for reasons known only to you, decided to help us. Tell us what those reasons are. Why are you helping us?"

Mandolin was taken off guard. He had expected an interrogation, not a soft inquiry into his motives for flipping. He lacked the emotional maturity and enlightenment to pause when taken by surprise. He did as he had always done; he blurted out the first thing that came to his head. "I work outside of the law but I'm no traitor."

When no one said anything he continued digging himself into a hole. "I'm not afraid of prison—I kill men and make it look like they've never been born. But I won't work for el diablo."

Serena studied Mandolin. She noted the religious tattoos and the large cross pendant on the chain around his neck. She thought, *say what you want about criminals, but sometimes their moral compass and loyalty are a*

cut above the average law-abiding citizen.
"Mandolin, who is 'the devil'?"

Mandolin searched her face for signs that she was pulling his leg. He snorted. "He's a CIA spook—I know it."

Serena put this piece of the puzzle on the table and tried to fit it with the other pieces that they already had. Something slid into place. "Did you talk to any of them?"

"El diablo is the whitest man I ever saw and his hair is redder than hers." He pointed to Jo.

Despite Mandolin drawing Jo into the conversation no one interrupted Serena, as they were all mesmerized by watching her work; even Agent Estep was paying attention. They sensed that she was leading up to something, but no one knew what it was. "Did the red-haired devil have a funny way of talking?"

Mandolin's facial expression told her the answer before he said it aloud. "Oh yeah. That spook isn't from here. El diablo, chica." He let the interrogation end on that note. After weighing his options, Mandolin decided that it was in his best interest not to disclose that he had a tracking device on the devil's vehicle and knew exactly where he was.

Natalie Buske Thomas

24

Serena was suited up, but she wasn't expecting any fanfare at the landing pad, which was a relief. Her initial awe about the ability to time-travel had waned. Today, Ruby Red was simply a mode of transportation. The absurd, the bizarre, the tacky, and the disgraceful – all of the cases she had investigated in the past flooded through her mind. She had empathy for Ann Kinji, who felt that she could never leave the

Presidency even after becoming a private citizen again.

Serena's impressive new career as a time-traveling detective was in many ways nothing more than a continuation of what she had always done. Humiliation and misunderstanding followed her like a dark cloud. Her humor was often misinterpreted as incompetence. She was judged to be vulgar by some and classy by others, and she had no idea on which side she would land. During her forty-four years on Earth she hadn't mastered how to project her true self to people. No matter how far she had come, she was always going to be that strange girl on the playground with the disturbing imagination.

Serena suddenly felt silly wearing her leather pilot's hat and green scarf. What had once been whimsical was now a farce. If not for the fact that the pilot's hat was hiding bed-head hair she would have removed it. She caught a glimpse of herself in the control panel mirror. A sad twelve-year old face stared back at her – she was the girl who was bored to tears by playing house with the girl gaggle on the playground. She was the girl who couldn't bear to read books about princesses. She wanted a tree house where she could escape the twitter of the gaggle and read boys' books about time travel. Didn't the middle-aged Serena owe it to her twelve-year-old self to appreciate the glory of this blessing? Serena was the world's first official time-traveler (not counting the scientists' and crew members' test-runs). *This is an amazing accomplishment*, she told herself. By the time the crew was ready to launch, Serena Wilcox had turned her attitude around.

This time Serena wasn't going into the past alone, nor was she headed there with only unarmed Jo at her side. No, the level of danger and intensity was out of her league. The idea of training Serena to be a one-woman army was ridiculous. Besides, the idea that she could take on an entire military operation alone would be too much for even a fantasy warrior princess, let alone a real person. Gender made no difference either. The unfriendly population was too large for any one person. They didn't have any concept of the numbers of enemies that they were up against, only that there were indeed enemies who had infiltrated Project Scarecrow. That hypothesis had been tested and proven to be true. Now they all realized that this had been the easy part.

Today's mission was destined to be gruesome. They were journeying to World War 1, the Meuse-Argonne offensive of October 1918. This point in history had been previously outside the boundaries of their time window. After Eduardo obtained the data from the orphanage in 1939 he effectively enlarged the time window to enable the men of the future to travel further into the past to this day, a critical turning point of World War 1. Serena assumed that the Meuse-Argonne offensive was important to whatever it is that MOTF (men of the future) were up to. No matter how daunting this mission was, armchair investigation was impossible: this time there was no getting around the need for Serena to travel to the battleground.

Serena had been an Army spouse during the early years of her marriage to Tom, but she'd never been in military service herself. Entering a combat zone was not something that she took lightly, and Tom was against it to the point of giving GSI an ultimatum: either he was part of the crew or she wasn't going. What

297

he could possibly do to protect her, she didn't know, and neither did anyone else. But everyone indulged in Tom's wish to be present on the battlefield.

Nothing about the way that GSI had operated thus far was conventional. With no firm protocol in place, and with an alarming according-to-Estep reliance on the quirky methods of blithe Serena, why pick this time to worry about rules or professionalism? And so it was that Tom was traveling with the crew, with Estep's objections duly noted but promptly disregarded.

Serena and the crew arrived safely in France with no molecules left behind. The concern about this was probably all in their heads, but several of them were obsessed with the possibility of a horrible accident resulting in a DNA scramble. Today's mission was to learn why MOTF wanted Eduardo to program the bands for this specific time and place. If they got lucky, they would also find and detain them, but no one expected to accomplish that stretch goal.

Their imaginations had conjured up images of futuristic warriors with weapons that vaporized people on sight. Their only hope was that the numbers worked in their favor – would MOTF send more than the two guys that they sent to Iowa? Were they watching Serena and GSI right now and countering their every move and had therefore amassed a small army?

Their fears about combating an army from the future were set aside as the reality of World War 1 set in. Whatever danger lay ahead with MOTF was temporarily unimportant. What was plainly obvious to them at that moment was that staying alive in the *past* was their first priority. Fears of fighting against men from the future would have to be put on hold for now. Serena had done some quick reading about the Meuse-Argonne offensive. However, nothing could have prepared her for the reality of being there.

She fleetingly wished that a cloak of invisibility had been possible, but unlike the physics of time travel, invisibility still existed only as a fictional superpower. The best they could do was to try to blend in. With such a large group this time around, Serena had her doubts that they could pull this off.

The clothes that they brought with them might not be enough to disguise that they didn't belong in this time period. What would happen when people from 1918 heard them speak? Nonetheless Serena donned a nurse's uniform, as did Jo. Everyone else on this mission was male, and all but Tom were outfitted as soldiers. Tom dressed as an Army chaplain. Putting that uniform on choked him with emotion. He could barely button himself up.

Natalie Buske Thomas

25

France 1918 was a challenging destination to program. Eduardo scheduled an emergency meeting with military history scholars as well as map experts and even a couple of retired generals. They met in clandestine fashion which suited them well. Several of Eduardo's picks hadn't been called into service for over a decade. Chomping at the bit to feel important again, they talked over each other and bickered at every turn.

"What do they want with the Meuse-Argonne offensive?" asked one of the generals.

"I told you, we don't know," said Eduardo.

"Sending them in without a clear mission is suicide," the general scoffed.

"We'll have to assume that they want to be in the heart of the action," offered one of the scholars.

"Look into 'open warfare' doctrine. Combine it with trench warfare. That was the winning strategy, and how the American army didn't let the Germans regroup," said another scholar.

Eduardo raised his voice over the now-overlapping conversations as each of the scholars was deeply engaged with generals and map experts in two separate tangents. "Stop, stop. Please." He waited until he had their attention before continuing. "You're misunderstanding what we're doing. We're trying to avoid combat."

One of the generals became indignant. "What the hell are we doing here then? I don't go to damn tea parties!"

Everyone laughed, which broke the ice somewhat. Eduardo attempted to smooth things over. "Our mission is surveillance in a heavy war zone. We want to minimize any possibility of discovery. And we want our people in and out without a scratch. I called you in here, General, because I trust that you have expertise for how to sneak up upon enemy lines in a surprise attack. In this case, we don't want an attack."

The general grunted. "I'm listening."

Eduardo's face was glossy with perspiration. "Our mission is to find out why the men of the future want to visit

World War 1. We are spying on the enemy in a battleground, not knowing what side our enemy is on, or what their purpose for being there is whatsoever. Are they there to observe or participate? We have no clue."

The same brusque voice piped up, "Are you telling me, young man, that these men of the future might aim to turn the fate of World War 1 against the Allies? If our boys are in trouble, it don't matter a damn if it's troops from today or yesterday or 19-damn-18. Send them what they need."

Eduardo smiled. He hadn't been called "young man" in a long time. He said, "I assume then that you'll help."

The general grunted, but he also nodded.

Everyone took their cue from him. The room immediately erupted into babble and a battle over who would lead the discussion. Tangents got them off track for hours. One scholar insisted on warning them of the risk of illness or death.

"If you had lived in the early twentieth century, your life expectancy would have been only fifty-three years. Influenza, pneumonia, tuberculosis and gastrointestinal infections killed Americans at an alarming rate. What's to prevent the crew from falling victim to one of these highly communicable diseases that were so rampant in 1918?"

Eduardo waved his hand. "We don't expect them to mingle with the populace."

"I'm not talking about the general populace. I'm talking about the crew's exposure to the troops. After the draft was implemented, American men were sent to military camps. These camps were a breeding ground for diseases like smallpox, dysentery, syphilis, and cholera. In 1918, American soldiers were among the earliest victims of the influenza pandemic. By the time Germany collapsed and peace was declared, nine million people, three hundred and forty thousand of them Americans, had died during the war. Compare that staggering statistic to the fifty million who would die in the influenza pandemic."

One of the map experts said, "A flu vaccine should take care of the problem."

This naïve comment incited full-out belly laughs from the scholarly section of the room. Everyone else was quiet; lacking any notion about why the vaccination idea wasn't valid. Someone explained, "The CDC can't produce a vaccine from the exact strain of flu that the crew may or may not be exposed to."

Eduardo shut down that conversation with the comment, "There's nothing we can do about the things we can't control."

The map expert, not discouraged by his poorly received suggestion about the flu vaccine, offered up another idea. "We can pray."

This led to one of the generals, who up until now had not uttered a word, standing and bowing his head. The others followed suit. This general led a windy prayer that addressed every conceivable concern that might befall the crew and the troops and the world at large. When the last "Amen" was spoken, a second general saluted an imaginary flag. The Pledge of Allegiance was said with conviction. When the room burst forth with the singing of the national anthem, more than one man shed tears.

Eduardo felt certain that he would lose his mind before all of the pent-up patriotic feelings of the old war heroes were depleted. But finally his agenda to pull together a realistic mission plan seemed possible. Sated by their emotional display of loyalty to God and country, their previous chatter gave way to productive dialogue.

Within minutes they settled on the Argonne forest for a landing. The dense forest was the most likely place to pop in without notice, though that choice was also wrought with peril. First, there was the problem of access in and out. There were only two passable roads in the area of the Allies' advance and even if they managed to make it past numerous booby traps to either of the roads, both were continuously exposed to German artillery fire. After they succeeded in getting the crew in, how could they get them back out?

Being trapped in the Argonne forest for the duration of their mission was unacceptable, as it was unlikely that the men of the future would reveal themselves in their exact chosen spot. They needed to move away from the combat zone as the mission led them. However, mobility outside of the forest was a puzzle that they laid aside. They focused on getting the crew into the combat zone. How they got themselves out of there was left up to them.

Fortunately all of their expert pre-planning and debate had paid off. The generals had mellowed after their egos were satisfied, and after their emotional impromptu prayer and song service they were astonishingly cooperative. In short order their landing strategy was planned to the utmost detail. GPS coordinates were created for the crew to maneuver through the Argonne and even throughout 1918 France as a whole, just in case. After that, the men were reluctant to wrap up their work on what had evolved into Operation Scarecrow, but Eduardo had no further need for their expertise.

He programmed the crew's materialization in the Argonne forest based on the location the experts had selected. The landing couldn't have gone more perfectly. The forest hid them completely; no one was concerned about being seen or heard.

It was what the crew should do *next* that was the issue. The experts never could agree on an exit strategy. Nor did they provide the crew with much training. The military history experts cited that General Pershing had to work with the army that he had, and not the army that he wished he had. He didn't wait for more training and neither should they. Like the enemies of World War 1, the crew's enemies—the mysterious men of the future—weren't going to wait for them to be ready for warfare. No, just like with Pershing's young raw American troops, the crew should enter the war zone with grit and fortitude. The right attitude could make up for a lot of deficiencies.

This particular advice fell on deaf ears. Of course the crew would receive training! They had state of the art training grounds and with special ops to work with, they could expedite training, working several days without much sleep if necessary. With time travel technology they could even bend time a little if they had to— though only as a last resort, as the time they played with still aged them. In this way, with every instance in which they paused time, they reduced the life expectancy of the time travelers. One day here, another day there, meant one less day to love and be loved. It meant one less day that the crew was meant to have lived. Any stoppage of time was therefore taken seriously, but then again, if they could prevent an untimely death in the field it was worth doing.

Besides the intense warfare training for combat circa 1918, involving only special ops (or the "Extreme A Team" as Beav had christened them), the entire crew took a crash course in navigation. Knowing where to go was not the same thing as knowing how to get there. Although the crew was supplied with GPS coordinates to merge with General Pershing's American troops, it was imperative that they were confident in finding their way in nearly blind conditions. The terrain was impenetrable with dense fog and heavy downpours that had saturated the Argonne forest.

Besides what nature had thrown at them, the Germans had toiled for years to make the vast forest impregnable. They had built concrete dugouts and machine gun bunkers. They had built fortified trench lines. And throughout it all they had planted hundreds of miles of barbed wire

314

that was nearly invisible beneath the overgrowth.

And when they did finally merge with the American troops of 1918, what then? It was highly unlikely that young, mostly untrained, soldiers in a combat zone environment would take notice of unfamiliar faces. The crew took precautions anyway. They rubbed mud on their faces to disguise their features and to hide their suspiciously clean skin. They did the same thing to their fresh uniforms. The ground had been drenched by unrelenting rainfall. Finding mud to smear on their bodies was an easy task.

After this mudding procedure, Agent Estep and his team were ready to roll out. They were better prepared and more experienced than the troops that they were merging with. Of the nine divisions from 1918, only four had seen combat. An alarming number of new recruits had never handled a rifle before stepping foot in France.

In contrast, the Extreme A Team was trained to handle unconventional high-risk missions in Special Forces. Their emergency crash training served only to educate them on what combat was like during the Meuse-Argonne Offensive. To blend, they carried replicas of weapons used during World War 1, but Beav had insisted that modern technology be built inside the casing. He assured them that no one would know from looking at the outside of the gun that the inner workings were light years ahead of their 1918 counterparts.

The Allied front assigned to the American Army was twenty-two miles wide and was comprised of fifteen infantry divisions and one cavalry division. The Extreme A Team was especially interested in the whereabouts of The First Army, commanded by General Pershing. They had hoped to catch a glimpse of the famous leader. However, the unrelenting rain would have made a Pershing sighting difficult, even if they had known where to find him. While the quest to find Pershing was squashed, their bravado was not dimmed in the slightest, not even when steady rain on their steel helmets produced nagging headaches within minutes of putting them on. Armed to the teeth and with enough testosterone to flood the forest, the Extreme A Team set off.

Serena, Jo and Tom were left floundering, but at least they had had the benefit of tapping into an enormous collection of military history resources dedicated to WW1. They had prepared their strategy ahead of time, zeroing in on Germany's "Scorched Earth Policy".

The Germans had burned entire towns and villages to the ground in an effective effort to slow down the advance of the Allied troops. This created impassable roads and a polluted water supply. After rain was added to this mess, as well as the danger of booby traps, sometimes the troops were without rations for an extended period of time. The need for rations gave the crew an opportunity.

Back home, Beav had put together rations with the help of theater design professionals. It was important that nothing about the packaging or the contents of the rations looked out of the ordinary for the time period. Their cover story: due to the hardships created by the Scorched Earth Policy, humanitarian aid had to be hand-delivered via combat nurses (Serena and Jo) and Army chaplains (Tom).

Their cover story was flimsier than they would have liked. The success of this plan relied upon the probability that the soldiers' relief at seeing rations would override any curiosity about who they were. Assuming that they did manage to blend in with the troops, the rest of their plan involved slipping out of the forest with the wounded. Even after they had consulted experts, the crew had never found a way out of the Argonne. Their only option was to attach themselves to American troops who had already established a proven method of getting people out.

Tom led Serena and Jo through the Argonne. They were ever mindful of barbed wire and other booby traps as they struggled to wade through the muck. Serena noticed camouflaged platforms in the trees on posts, like structures that a deer hunter might use, except that the purpose of these platforms was to hunt humans. The posts were abandoned today, thank God.

They made it through the mud, avoiding all traps and hazards, and met up with the first unit that they could find. No cover story was necessary. As soon as one of the soldiers spied the uniformed trio he shouted, "Over here!"

There was a flurry of activity as the troops parted to clear a path for Tom, Serena and Jo to follow. The purpose of this became obvious as they drew near. The most heartbreaking and hideous sounds would haunt their ears forever.

Young men—no, boys—were screaming and crying out in anguish, thrashing and seizing on the ground. Wet from the pelting rain, their uniforms were stuck fast to their skin. The mud coated their clothing in a thick mat. The overall effect was that these mere children seemed naked, soaked down to their skin, covered with their own blood and excrement.

The boy soldier who had been standing guard over the wounded fell to his knees when he saw Serena and Jo. "God has sent me angels," he breathed.

The two women looked nothing like angels in their period piece "outdoor" nursing uniforms consisting of a hat that looked more suitable for a safari vacation than for patching up soldiers, a waterproof trench coat and gloves. Outdoor nursing corps uniforms had been issued in 1917 when nurses were ordered to Europe to serve in base, evacuation, and mobile surgical hospitals, and to provide care on hospital trains and transport ships. These uniforms were required not only for convenience and necessity, but also for purposes of identification of corpses, a fact that Serena didn't want to think about. Serena and Jo's severe dark trench coat and hat made them look less like angels

321

and more like private eyes, but they were nonetheless angels to this soldier.

Jo grabbed Serena by the wrist and leaned down to whisper in her ear, "I can't do this."

Serena turned to face Jo. "You're stronger than you think you are." Then she switched off the part of her brain that registered emotions. The same qualities that Serena had been often criticized for; her callousness, her brevity during intense situations, and her flippant attitude toward life in general, were the very qualities that made her exactly the right person to show up at a time like this.

She sprang into action, sizing up who was most in need of attention. She had few supplies on her, but fortunately her cover as a nurse meant that she had an emergency first aid kit. Not only that, but their production team didn't have time to prepare a vintage true-to-history kit. They found only a bag suitable for the time period. The actual medical supplies were bursting with modern day miracles. These young soldiers knew nothing about medicine and were none the wiser that her nursing supplies were from over a hundred years into the future.

Serena patched up the soldiers the best that she could, relying on her years of patching up her kids and her experience in serving as her mother's caregiver. *In a pinch, anyone can be a nurse*, she thought. *It's about doing what needs to be done.*

Nonetheless, she was too out of her depth to do a proper job with these young men. She lacked skills, training, and medical school, not to mention that, although they had used whatever they could to elevate them from the flooded soil, these soldiers needed a sterile environment as soon as possible. Serena told herself that her role was only to prepare the wounded for transporting. Real nurses would take care of the rest.

Jo was true to her word—she really couldn't do this. She had turned even whiter than her Irish skin already was and had fainted. There were plenty of takers to catch her before she fell. Since it was obvious that Jo wasn't going to be much use as a combat nurse, Serena tasked her instead with consoling the soldier who had stood guard over his wounded comrades.

Tom looked mighty green, as he too was squeamish around blood, but he held up well and he was her lifeline throughout the whole grisly affair. He assisted Serena by emptying both her pack and Jo's. He gave her supplies from the packs as needed. Most of all, he gave her reassurance and support with nothing more than one meaningful look with his sky blue eyes.

Serena's stint as a combat nurse was over within the half hour. All twenty-three of the wounded soldiers were cleaned up, sanitized and bandaged with an efficiency that wasn't yet possible in 1918. She had cheated by using supplies that were from her present day world. She cringed when she realized that she may have altered history by saving someone who was meant to die. But when she looked into their young faces she knew that she wouldn't have done it any differently even if she had been mindful of the risks.

The wounded were lifted by stretchers out of the combat zone. They were transported through a tedious route that got them safely to the battalion first aid station. Serena, Tom and Jo stayed on with the wounded. The soldiers who had carried their fallen comrades through the Argonne forest returned to their positions on the frontlines. Serena wished that she could

325

make these solider boys stay with her. One of them looked to be the same age as her own son, who was probably asleep in his nice warm bed at home, wearing his favorite Superman sleep pants instead of an Army uniform.

Serena put the brakes on those thoughts before homesickness derailed her. She focused on the twenty-three wounded soldiers she had helped to save. First they were labeled with tags that were tied to their bodies. The tags stated their rank, their name, their injury, and where they were from.

Next, the decision was made about where to send them. Serena was proud that there was no need for the soldiers to stop first at the Regimental Dressing Station, as their wounds were declared "sufficiently dressed" for the 4.5 kilometer ambulance ride to the field hospital. It was a rather nasty ride over torn roads, but it was almost made up for when the men finally arrived at the hospital. They received warm sponge baths that were most welcome, especially since the nurses who attended to them were not much older than they were, and were the most beautiful girls they had ever laid eyes upon. The soldiers fell back down to earth when these same beauties gave them their tetanus shots.

With the soldiers' care now in more competent hands, Serena was ready to be reassigned to a less critical task. She didn't have long to wait. Serena and Jo were put to work almost immediately in a different area of the field hospital. Their job was to prepare cards to attach to the "human baggage", an unfortunate term that the soldiers had assigned themselves. The cards served as records for transfer soldiers and were required to be worn at all times. After the soldiers were carded they were then loaded for transport to another facility. Some were destined for an evacuation hospital, such as an old French barracks. Others were headed for the train.

It was while attaching the record cards that Serena and Jo had the opportunity to talk with the soldiers. They didn't fear that their futuristic tongues would ring any alarm bells. They blended in easily with the mishmash of diverse accents in the ward and they were confident that they would be assumed to be from "somewhere else" like everyone else there was. It wasn't hard to get the soldiers talking and once they started talking, Serena was able to deduce what the men of the future were doing in 1918.

Several of the soldiers couldn't wait to describe the strange things they saw on the battlefield. Serena and Jo listened to everyone's stories, and then asked three of the soldiers to go over their accounts in more detail. Serena didn't remember their first names or their military ranks and could later recall them only by their last names: Crandal, Frank, and Thompson. She did remember their faces, and the stories they told about their hometowns.

Frank had a girl back home. He showed them a well-worn picture of a pretty young woman in a white dress. Crandal was from the deep South. His drawl was challenging to decipher. Thompson was a Yankee through and through. He was almost as impossible to understand as Crandal. So it was Frank they relied on the most to tell them what happened.

Frank said, "I never saw anything like it. We were shot at by a German machine-gun nest at the top of a hill. The guns were spitting fire and I didn't have time to run or hide. I did the only thing I could do, I kept firing. And they kept firing. This went on and on. We cut down the Germans who popped their heads up over the hill. They cut down some of us too. This went on for an eternity until Hitler sent the bump in the night."

Crandal hijacked the story. His eyes were open wide, and combined with the appearance of his stark white hair, he looked like a ghost had frightened all the color out of him. "Lights were flashing. Then men were disappearing on my left and on my right. I'd look over and they'd be done. I heard nothing but the sound of helmets hitting mud."

Thompson added, "The only things left were their clothes. The bodies were gone."

26

Mandolin was free and clear, even though he had committed murder for hire: GSI had made him an asset. He understood that his status could be revoked at any time and off to prison he would go. His choices were to play ball or to make a run for the border. But he also knew that GSI had the backing of the full United States government and would hunt him down to the end of his days—escape

331

was not a viable option. Between life in prison without the possibility of parole or steady work with a comfortable paycheck, was there really a choice? He didn't hesitate to sign his life away to GSI. Besides, Mandolin had grown weary of being on the wrong side of the law.

In addition to Mandolin, every man on his payroll had also received immunity. The same terms applied. They would either fly straight or go to jail. And so it was that Mandolin had a job for the unforeseeable future and he was even able to retain his own people.

Ann Kinji had surmised that Mandolin's way of doing things had been efficient and effective when he was working for the villains—why wouldn't he be equally effective if he applied his system toward working for the good guys? She theorized that she didn't need more people who were trained to think like agents. She needed assets who thought like criminals.

This utilization of criminals as assets wasn't exactly her original idea; she had borrowed it from Serena's use of the criminally insane during Operation Covert Coffee, and of course the CIA had been doing it since inception. Ann had a gut feeling that this strategy would be effective for Project Scarecrow, or Operation Scarecrow, depending on whether she was looking at it from the civilian or from the military perspective.

Mandolin's first mission was to track the mysterious MOTF, the red-headed devil himself. He still hadn't given GSI full disclosure; they didn't know that Mandolin already knew where the man was. Why not let GSI think that he was a brilliant tracker? He chuckled to himself, knowing how easy it was going to be to "find" the MOTF, an acronym that he had personally reassigned from "men (or man) of the future" to a vulgar two-word phrase befitting of the man he was approaching at this very moment.

The devil didn't hear Mandolin's feather-light right-hand man approaching. Slim Jim, as he was known in Mandolin's circles, was as stealthy as humanly possible. Superstitious members of Mandolin's posse believed that Slim Jim's stealth went beyond human constraints. The MOTF apparently had no special powers to detect Slim Jim's presence because he was taken completely off guard.

Slim Jim used old school chloroforming on the devil and the MOTF slumped immediately into Jim's arms. Mandolin rushed to assist. Slim Jim had come by his name honestly; he lacked the heft to wrangle a big man like the MOTF. The task was no obstacle for Mandolin. He tucked the unconscious man alongside him like a ragdoll and hustled him into their getaway vehicle without anyone seeing a thing.

They arrived at GSI through the employee entrance, shielded from the public lobby area. An agent met Mandolin at the door to transfer the MOTF via wheelchair to the investigative wing of the Gödel Solution Institute. The investigative wing contained several interrogation rooms, a library, a computer lab, and a recreation room for the agents to dine, relax, and even sleep. The room had been designed by the agents themselves and included a high-tech coffee maker.

The MOTF was wheeled into Interrogation Room B and immediately cuffed. No one wanted a repeat of what had been named "The Eduardo Snafu" almost as soon as the incident occurred. The agents' fondness for labels, acronyms and insider jokes created an atmosphere of cronyism that Mandolin was not yet a part of, and perhaps would never be a part of. Besides, he was only an asset, tasked with specific jobs. No one trusted him with the inner workings of GSI. Indeed, he and his posse had to submit to receiving a tracking implant on condition of their freedom.

Today was Mandolin's last day of involvement in Project Scarecrow, but he was confident that GSI would call upon him again in the near future. When another job came up that required his unique skill set, they'd think of him. Their people smelled of government. When baby-faced suits didn't fit the bill, he knew that they'd call upon craggy, massive, scarred and tattooed Mandolin. The fact that he was also Latino was a racist criterion, that he was aware of and offended by, but he knew that he brought something to the table that the other agents couldn't. So while Mandolin was dismissed for now, he knew that they needed him. He'd be back.

After Mandolin exited the premises GSI was dark except for the lone cluster of lights in the upper level investigation wing and the secret service detail on every floor of the building. There was a huddle around the coffee maker as the crew and the Extreme A Team filled their mugs. No one spoke until Ann Kinji gestured for them to sit around the table.

The table had been brought in from the board room where many of them had worked together on Operation Covert Coffee during Ann's presidency. The table that they had developed a fondness of had been gifted to GSI by the new administration, here in the flesh with them now. Mr. President, Joseph Smythe had missed the launch and all of the other public relations events for GSI. He was at the Gödel Solution Institute for the first time under a cloak and dagger arrangement. He had no interest in taking a tour of the facility or warming up the room with preliminary small talk. He and Ann had a compatible style of getting straight to the point. He got to the point now.

"Thank you for welcoming me here today…" He frowned when his words created a flurry of motion. "No standing ovation. Sit. We have work to do. As your Commander in Chief I need my own eyes and ears on Project Scarecrow. Ann informs me that this has become a military operation that has unfortunately caused our diligent civilians here to be drafted into combat. This is beyond unacceptable. I don't even know what to say." He placed his arms on the table, folded his hands, and pressed his forehead on this clasped fingers. No one knew if he was praying or thinking, or both of these. He remained in this position for a long stretch of time

338

while everyone grew restless from the wait. President Smythe was a man who hurried for no one. When he released his meditative state he looked down the table at Jo. "You could have been killed, my dear." And almost as an afterthought he addressed Serena Wilcox. "And you as well."

Amused expressions were on all of their faces. Ann yanked that carpet out from under all of them. "Joe, I've said it before and I'll say it again. Marry the girl. No one likes a bachelor President."

The agents and crew felt the uncomfortable heat and looked at their feet, the ceiling—anywhere else but at the President. Jo flushed crimson. Everyone held their breath until they heard President Joseph Smythe laugh. He said, "Fair enough. But I don't think she'd like it much if I proposed right now."

Serena joked, "When you do propose, watch out. She's a fainter."

Joe smiled. "Thank you for giving me a transition back on track, Ms. Wilcox. Yes, fainting. I heard that it was a gruesome ordeal for Jo, Serena and Tom both on the battlefield and then later at the field hospital. That should have never happened. What did you even gain from that experience that could possibly justify you being there?"

Serena offered, "It was mandatory, Mr. President. The mission cracked the case wide open. If not for what the soldiers told us in the field hospital, I don't think we'd be as close as we are to figuring out what the men of the future are up to."

Joe placed his fingers together like a steeple. "Enlighten me. I read the report, but I want to hear it straight from you. But before you launch into this, how is Tom doing? No post-traumatic stress I hope. I heard that he had to give last rites to dozens of soldiers at the hospital."

Serena sighed. "He said it was the hardest thing he's ever had to do in his life. Some of those boys were the same age as our own son. But Beav and the others had prepped him well for the task and Tom did as he was trained to do. He'll be OK. He might keep me up all night with his thrashing, but he'll move on from this, eventually."

Joe scowled. "That's most unfortunate. So convince me, Serena, that this mission was at all necessary."

"Of course it was necessary. The soldiers opened up to us in a way that they weren't likely to have done with agents. Jo and I were their nurses. We were easy to confide in. And what they had to say was exactly the type of information that we were looking for. It's all in the report."

Joe grabbed the report packet, lifted it a few inches from the table and then deliberately let it drop. The loud smack when the packet hit the tabletop jolted everyone. "I know what's in the report. I won't make up my mind until I hear it straight from you."

Serena didn't intimidate easily, but Mr. President Joe was not the affable and downright goofy man that she knew from working with him on Operation Covert Coffee when he was still Speaker of the House. This Joe was commanding in a way that made her want to straighten up her act. All of her playfulness, flippancy and impishness drained from her. She answered the question.

"The soldiers told us that they had seen strange things on the battlefield. People were getting zapped into thin air. One minute their comrade was by their side in the trenches and the next, poof!

Gone. Nothing left but their clothes. It was soundless. The only noise was the sickening thump when the uniform and helmet fell. Their ears caught on to that thump right away and associated the sound with the casualty. The soldiers described it as the bump in the night. They don't believe this to be the work of an otherworldly being. They believe that Hitler arranged it."

Joe cleared his throat. "And you say that this information couldn't have been obtained some other way? You are the only one who could have uncovered this?"

Serena glanced at her feet. "I wouldn't say I'm the only one. But someone had to speak directly to the soldiers and they weren't going to be forthcoming if the approach wasn't right. None of them seemed willing to go on record. They were terrified. I don't think Special Forces or agents would have gotten very far. They

343

would have likely denied seeing anything at all."

Joe turned his attention to Beav. "And you were here on the home front. Production team it says." He opened the packet and flipped through the folder to find the page he was looking for. "You supplied everyone with the training and supplies that they needed, and arranged COM with Lehman?"

Beav and Lehman said, "Yes, Mr. President." Their voices were not in unison, but instead Beav's voice awkwardly trailed behind Lehman's.

Joe nodded. "That seems straightforward." He put Agent Estep on the hot seat next. "You are the one with the most to explain. From what I gather, you've been out there playing cowboy."

"I wouldn't say that," said Estep.

Everyone looked to Ann to interject. She said, "I wouldn't say that either, but

344

Joe has the floor. I asked him to approach this any way that he needed. Sorry, but I'm leaving you all hanging out to dry. If your work holds up, you'll emerge from this just fine. If it doesn't, you don't deserve my protection anyway."

Serena quipped, "This is 'bad cop, bad cop'." As soon as she said those words she regretted it. She felt the glares from dozens of pairs of eyes on her back.

Joe snapped his fingers. "Estep, on with it. Defend your actions."

Estep balked for a second before resigning himself into submission. "I did what I thought was best, Sir. Ms. Wilcox and Jo couldn't walk into a combat zone without support. I personally didn't think that this mission was wise from the get-go; I'd never have sent them in there. But I did what I could with what I was assigned to do. I knew that this operation was beyond the scope of what my team was trained for.

I needed military support, Special Forces even. I spoke behind closed doors with a retired general who was able to make arrangements with prior military personnel available for hire. They are trained in special ops for private or private/government hybrids such as GSI."

Joe slid the folder across the table to land in front of Estep. "Explain why your team shot and killed thirteen German soldiers."

Estep's throat was parched but he dare not ask for water. "Collateral damage, Sir."

"Collateral damage? Explain how that term fits this situation."

"Sir, we were there to provide emergency rescue for Serena, Jo and Tom. In the process, we needed to blend in as soldiers. We didn't engage in battle directly. We only shot when fired upon."

Joe pointed his finger at Estep. "No!"

Estep was speechless.

Joe tapped his finger on the table. "No, you did not need to blend in. You didn't need to go anywhere near the front lines. You could have hung back. You could have climbed into the abandoned firing posts in the trees. You could have hidden yourselves in the Argonne forest so well that no one could have ever found you. You had special ops with you. They know how to disappear. There is no excuse for entering a World War 1 combat zone and, for reasons downright unfathomable to me, engage in warfare."

Estep swallowed. "Am I fired, Sir?"

Joe shook his head. "I don't know yet. I just don't know."

Serena raised her hand. "Can I ask Estep a question?"

Joe threw his hands up.

Serena took that as a yes. "Estep, did you see anything unusual?"

347

"You mean like vaporizing soldiers?"

"Yes. Was there anything at all like that? Was there any sign of futuristic weapons or anything at all that would indicate that the MOTF were there?"

Estep snorted. "If we'd seen anything like that, it would be in the report."

One of Estep's Extreme A Team members, a man known as "Runner" spoke up. "Actually, sir, I did see something. No one asked me."

All eyes shot to the special ops man in the back of the room. Runner continued. "I saw a streak of light. It was a flash, like from a camera. Then the German I had my sights on was gone. I thought nothing of it, figured I'd blinked. How he hid from view so fast, I can't explain. The cogs of war move on. I forgot about it until now."

Serena followed up. "Where was the flash originating from? Did you see who may have done this?"

"I think I did see. There was an American solider not more than, oh, about six or seven feet away from me when the flash went off and I lost sight of the German."

Serena pressed on, noting that no one was stopping her. "What made you think that the soldier next to you was a MOTF?"

"I didn't think that he was then. I'm only thinking of it now that I'm remembering the flash. It didn't register with me at the time that there was something off about him."

Serena prodded. "Off? How so?"

"His face was, I don't know, different. It was like he was of an ethnicity I'd never seen before. He talked funny too. I'm fluent in seven different languages and his accent was nothing I'd ever heard before."

Serena sat up straight. "Wait, he spoke to you? What did he say?"

"He wasn't talking to me." Runner glanced at Jo. "He said 'Take that, you, uh, SOB.'"

Silence fell. Joe let the quiet settle over them until the sounds of shuffling feet alerted him that it was time to move on. He stood. "I've heard all I needed to hear. I've made my decision."

Everyone blinked back at him in confusion. Jo asked what was on their minds, "Decision about what? About Estep?"

Joe shook his head. "About the continued use of untrained civilians, and about the need for Serena Wilcox—is she a sideshow or an investigator? What is my beloved Jo doing in a place like this?"

Ann clacked her tongue. "Disregard the words 'my beloved'. Joe, no more flirting. I don't care if you are the President of the United States. I'm older than you I'll put you in time out."

Joe shrugged. "She's right. I'm out of control. I'll resolve that with you later, Jo."

Jo couldn't meet anyone's eyes. They didn't know if she was mortified by the attention, or by Joe's pursuit of her. Ann Kinji was right, the situation was distracting. They were relieved when Joe moved on.

"Like I said, I've made my decision. Agent Estep, I made you sweat and I don't regret doing so. You were out of line. You can't mess with history. You can't take lives. And Ms. Wilcox, you can't save lives either. I'd declare the Argonne mission a disaster if not for the fact that you did deliver on your investigation. We now know that men of the future are interfering with points in history. We have multiple eyewitness accounts, heard directly from the lips of the solders from 1918 and from our own soldier in the room with us as I speak. These eyewitness accounts bring the truth to light instantly. There's no faster way to the truth than to go to the battle in person and see it with your own eyes and ears. It is for this reason that I do see value in what Ms. Wilcox contributes. Her unorthodox ways have an uncanny way of getting her at the right place at the right time. I suspect that Ms. Wilcox is a ringer. Don't let the silliness fool you—I took a peak at her entrance exam. Perhaps you didn't know that the exam is an IQ test. But then again, with a score as high as yours is, you probably knew that and somehow gamed the system. Whatever you are, you are an enigma for sure. And you do get results. It might be a contorted ride to get to what we need to know, but you do get us there. Serena stays on, and she can continue to have whatever she wants. But there is a big change effective immediately."

Ann stepped forward from where she had been leaning against the wall by the door. "We are in agreement on this."

Joe continued. "We need to keep the Extreme A Team permanently and officially employed—that means based and housed on site at GSI, consider this to be a hybrid military. But we need more training, in effect ASAP. We need for Agent Estep to understand that the number one objective on these missions is to stay hidden. You are there for emergency evacuations only. If I thought that any one of you could handle what Serena does, I'd much rather that all future time travel be done solely by agents and soldiers. But this is unchartered territory and I believe that the only one in this room with outside-of-the-box thinking far enough outside of the box to encompass all of time and space is Serena Wilcox Bridges."

Ann smiled. "Agreed. That's why she's here."

Serena decided to speak up. "I've been evaluated time and time again. When will this exercise stop?"

"Never," said Ann. "All of you are under constant and perpetual observation and evaluation. Anyone can be let go at any time. What is it that you think I do around here? The Gödel Solution Institute isn't a sci-fi reality show for the social media channel. Lest you forget, time travel belongs to the world. We are pioneering in waters that could flood the time space continuum if we screw up. If we leave one faucet on, if we break one pipe, if we stop up one toilet—we'll flood the universe."

27

M r. President left with his secret service detail. GSI was even quieter now. What remained was potentially a long night ahead as they waited for the red-headed devil to wake up. Slim Jim had knocked him out too heavily. The wait for him to regain consciousness was wearisome. The crew hit the coffee maker for another round.

They settled into the lounging area and several of them nodded off. About an hour later Beav came back with news. "He's come to."

They clustered around Interrogation Room B, everyone pressed against the glass even though there was ample seating space for all. Only Serena and Beav went inside the room. Serena studied the man she saw in front of her before taking a seat across from him at the interrogation table. The MOTF was a bland looking man. His features were so nondescript that they seemed genderless, like a generic storefront mannequin head might look. There was too much chisel and perfection in his face. This was either the result of plastic surgery or selective genetics. The overall effect was what Runner had described: the man's features seemed to be of an unknown ethnicity.

Serena began. "Let me introduce myself. I'm…"

"Serena Wilcox Bridges, wife to Tom Bridges, mother of three children, former private detective, time traveler, and nuisance."

Serena was taken aback. She recovered nicely and plowed through. "You already know me then. So how have I been a nuisance to you?"

The MOTF flexed his jaw. "The World Order canceled our project because of your meddling."

Beav stepped in. "Explain."

"She saved men who were meant to die. Her people killed men who were meant to live. What part of this do you not understand? We had to go back in and fix it."

"How did you do that? What did you do?" Serena pressed.

The MOTF leered at her. "That's beyond your intelligence and beyond my interest in helping you."

Beav scoffed. "There's no need to get snide. How far into the future are you from?"

"I'm not telling. Suffice it to say, you are pests, you pioneers of time travel technology. You have no concept of protocol. You have no idea how to harness the power."

Serena shrugged. "Fair enough. Can you at least tell us what you were doing in Argonne, during World War 1?"

"You've heard of Army simulation games? The skills of warfare need to be taught before a soldier enters the battlefield. This exercise reduces the incidence of PTSD and creates a better soldier."

Serena nodded. "Is that what you were doing there? Simulation games in real battle situations?"

"Yes. We targeted only those men who were meant to die. We were careful not to leave any evidence behind. Then you come crashing in, saving lives and taking lives that were not yours to decide. You screwed up the whole of the universe. We not only had to fix it, but we took the brunt of it as well. It is my people who are harmed by your actions. The entire simulation program has been canceled."

Serena analyzed her emotions. *Do I feel sympathy for this man? Should I?* She decided that there was something about this MOTF that she didn't trust and she didn't like. "You've made it clear that we acted irresponsibly and that we took lives that we were not meant to take. How do you explain your own actions, when you killed

Gentry, Jorgi, and probably several others as well? How is it that you can play God?"

The red-headed devil flicked his tongue over his lips, a tongue that was shockingly literally forked. He said, "Because you believe in God."

Serena felt a chill. "And you don't?"

"I didn't say that."

Beav asked the next question against his gut telling him not to. "Then what are you saying?"

The MOTF threw back his head, opened his mouth, and released his serpentine tongue. He hissed, "We have become equal with God."

Serena suddenly knew how Jo had felt when she had seen all of the blood and suffering. She felt her face grow white as a sheet. Her heart palpitated. She could scarcely breathe. When she found the strength to speak she uttered, "Get thee behind me Satan."

The MOTF laughed. "I'm not Satan! I'm humanity in a few dozen years."

Serena scolded herself for losing her cool. "You won't be going back to the snake hole you slithered out of. You killed people here and we'll hold you accountable for that."

He grinned. "You think you can hold me? I travel telepathically. I can teleport. Put it into words your monkey brain can understand. When your intelligence catches up you'll grasp the concept. But, oh that's right, you'll be long in the grave before then. I came for the wristbands because we needed to go back as far as 1918 and you hadn't supplied us with data that far back. We had to drop by and fetch it for ourselves. We came, we got what we wanted, and when I tire of talking to you, I'll leave."

Serena held up her hand. "You didn't get what you wanted. We stopped you from playing your war games with real people's lives. Those families deserved a body and a proper burial. Isn't vaporization a form of meddling? You fixed what we had screwed up and we fixed what you had screwed up. I'd call us even."

The MOTF spat directly into Serena's face. Had there not been glass between them, she would have been hit. Spittle ran down the glass. "If I see you again, you won't get out alive."

That threat was the last thing he said. He vanished immediately afterward. Serena jumped up right away and said, "Collect that saliva off the glass!" And for a few minutes they were distracted by this errand. But that energy wore off and the weight of what they had witnessed fell heavily upon them.

By the time Serena rejoined the crew she was rattled to the core. She stumbled about as the beaten soul that she was. Jo wrapped her arms around her. Malirah added her own arms. This group hug grew and grew until everyone was linked. Even Agent Estep and the Extreme A Team were added to the huddle. But it was when they noticed that Ann Kinji was quietly sobbing that they all lost control. One after another, not a single one of them had dry eyes. That's when Runner's voice rang out from somewhere inside the thirty-person clinch. "Dear Heavenly Father, please protect us from this evil. Amen."

28

Eduardo, Buick, Runner, Malirah, Jo, Lehman, Estep, Beav, Serena and Ann were in conference. These were the ten people chosen to wrap up the final report for the Gödel Solution Institute's first mission, Project Scarecrow. Eduardo had been a part of it from the beginning. Buick and Malirah had come on board several years later, right around the time when then-President Ann Kinji had an inkling that something about the project seemed more than what it appeared to be in the reports.

Beav, Jo, Estep and Serena didn't jump in until after GSI was already slated to investigate Project Scarecrow. New member Runner was joining them for the first time today. He was selected to join the crew after he showed initiative during yesterday's nerve wracking briefing with current President Joseph Smythe.

Runner was to lead the Extreme A Team, answering to Agent Estep. In this way, Estep had been assigned a confusing role of Federal Agent/Special Ops General. They decided to create a whole new entity to resolve this absurdity. Agent Estep was now in charge of the GSI Special Ops, or GSO. He had not quit his day job and insisted that he would remain a federal agent.

Beav complained, "We're getting lost in acronyms. This sounds more and more like a government institution every day. This isn't what I signed on for."

Estep said, "You're just saying that because no one gave you an acronym."

Ann grabbed a pencil from her desk drawer. She tapped the pencil but she didn't gnaw on the eraser. "Beav is right. GSI isn't what I expected it to be. But the Gödel Solution Institute has already done good work. The future is complicated and we're dealing with enemies with unknown power. It chills me to the bone to think about what they might be capable of. While this governmental structure isn't what I intended GSI to be, I assure you that I still own this company. I'm utilizing my influence to tap into government resources. We need this.

As much as I wish we could handle our operations independently, I'm afraid we are up against forces too great for us to handle without super-power backing. The Special Ops team? It's necessary. No, we didn't need it in Argonne, not to rescue our crew anyway. Instead, our Special Ops caused more harm than good.

But Runner witnessed something important, and the level of danger was high enough that Serena, Jo and Tom could have been killed that day. Of course we shouldn't be involved in combat zones again, but then again, what if we are? We aren't the ones choosing these missions.

We're trying to stay one step ahead, or at least chasing on the heels of, the MOTF, whoever they are. As it stands today, we still don't know. The DNA sample from the man we're calling 'the red-headed devil' gave us a bizarre result. We couldn't make heads or tails of it. It was as if he had scrambled his genetic material so as to be unidentifiable. I suppose that will one day happen—as the criminal element is easily found through DNA matches, it stands to reason that one day they will find a way around this. It looks like the MOTF have done exactly that."

"Are you saying that we'll be chasing these MOTF through time and space indefinitely?" asked Beav.

Serena said, "If we don't what's to stop them from erasing history? Why let GSI exist? Why not get rid of me?" She asked these somewhat hypothetical questions and then added, "Why am I not clever enough that my future self would give me a message to warn us?"

Beav laughed. "Well, if anyone could figure that out it would be…"

Everyone froze as the screens in the board room flickered. The red message light blinked on and off, on and off. No one breathed. Ann Kinji said, "You have

369

the digital pad on your side of the table, Serena. Who is it from?"

Serena stared at them in disbelief. "It's from me."